IN MY
BROTHER'S
SHADOW

In My Brother's Shadow

A Fantasy Novel

Lacey Leach

Palmetto Publishing Group, LLC
Charleston, SC

For information regarding special discounts for bulk purchases, please contact
Palmetto Publishing Group at Info@PalmettoPublishingGroup.com.

ISBN-13: 978-1-944313-64-7
ISBN-10: 1-944313-64-8

To my family and friends, especially my children,
and to Nathan, my lover, my best friend, and my greatest supporter.

PROLOGUE

"**D**amn it all to hell!"
The room suddenly fell silent. Tensions were high in the kingdom of Halcyon Ridge that day, and nowhere was this truer than in the King's council chamber. Twelve tall, burly men, typical Halcyonians, had convened in the topmost room of the castle's northwest tower, planning the best way to be rid of their enemies. One of the twelve was King Reginald Faircross, a youngster compared to his eleven trusted advisers.

At just twenty years old, the King had reluctantly ascended to the throne after the untimely death of his parents, who had been taken by the pox six months before. He had just been getting used to the title when a problem had arisen with one of the neighboring kingdoms. At the time, it had been miniscule, but had quickly escalated to a property dispute, and the two nations had been unable to agree upon a simple solution to their issues. Despite this, Reginald tried to make peace with the Marquis of Alamure; but when the peace was betrayed by an assassination attempt financed by the Marquis, the furious Reginald had immediately called their kingdoms to war. It wasn't what he wanted, but desperate times called for desperate measures.

Reginald stood atop the war table, his figures and maps laid out for everyone to see. Winning looked to be a lot harder than he had originally imagined. His kingdom was nestled amongst and surrounded by mountains, and Alamure had the upper hand in terms of men and resources.

"This isn't good," the young king muttered, fists clenched as he glared down at the table.

"Sire, what do you plan to do?"

The voice came from a mustachioed brown-haired man to his left; and as he turned toward the speaker, Reginald sighed heavily. "I don't know, Kameran... I suppose we have no choice but to go into battle with what we have. There's no turning back now."

"But Sire, that's suicide!" came an elderly voice from his right. Others began to chatter quietly about the dangers of this type of action.

Reginald's fists balled even tighter. "Enough!" His voice boomed over everyone else's, and once again silence filled the room. Reginald stood tall and put a hand upon his chin in thought. "It's the only way we can do this. I have faith in our troops," he said in a softer voice. Turning to Kameran, "Knight Captain, are you with me?"

The knight snapped to attention and bowed respectfully. "My liege, I would follow you anywhere."

Reginald's worried look faded into a small smile. "Good. Then get your men ready. We leave tomorrow."

The next day, the halls of the castle echoed to the fanfare outside the walls, and banners hung from every corner and window. Today was the day when Good King Reginald led his men into a war that would change the fate of their kingdom.

No one but the armor-clad soldiers and the king himself were inside the keep at the moment. In the company of his royal bodyguards, Reginald strode toward the Great Hall's doors in his gleaming golden armor. The throne room was empty; it was usually full of peasants or aristocrats, waiting to petition him. Unfortunately, that wasn't happening today, and he would miss that. He looked around, brushing dark brown hair out of his eyes as he did. Seeing that the preparations were almost complete, Reginald smiled and began to walk toward the exit.

Suddenly he stopped, hearing the patter of small feet behind him. He knew that it could only be one person, and he shook his head, smiling playfully. "Well, well. I guess he couldn't stay away, could he? Even after I told him to," the king murmured to himself.

"Reggie!" called the voice of a young boy. King Reginald turned to see a ten-year-old running up to him. As he reached the small entourage, the boy stopped before the king and leaned on his knees. "Reggie... Wait... Please..." he panted.

Reginald chuckled, kneeling down to him. "Dearest brother, what's wrong?" he asked.

The boy looked up at him and wrapped his slender arms around the King's neck. "Please don't go, Reggie... Why do you have to go?" he sobbed, tears in his eyes. Reginald was a bit startled, but he smiled gently and put his arm around his brother's shoulders.

"Because I'm the king, Gabriel. I must go. It's my sworn duty to protect the people," Reginald replied, giving his brother a heartfelt squeeze before standing again. Gabriel wiped his eyes with his sleeve, trying to be tough and not show his tears; but it was hard, because Reginald was the only family he had left. The king handed the boy a handkerchief, which Gabriel took quickly and wiped his face. Then Reginald tousled his brother's mahogany hair fondly and grinned. "Come now, you have to be strong! If I don't come back, *you* are going to have to be king."

Gabriel frowned hard. "But you're going to come back! You always do," he cried. "Promise me, Reggie, promise you'll come home safely!"

Reginald looked at his younger brother, surprised at his insistence. However, he smiled and held an armored pinky finger out to Gabriel, who took it in his own bare one. "I promise that no matter what happens, I will always be by your side, Prince Gabriel," Reginald swore. Gabriel smiled broadly as Reginald stood. "Now," the king continued, "Come with me."

Gabriel grinned cheekily and ran to the door to wait. Reginald muttered to himself, "Such enthusiasm..." He then followed his brother out into the castle courtyard, where the fanfare grew louder than ever.

Thousands upon thousands of people had gathered to watch their king ride off with his knights. Gabriel walked beside the King, grinning at Reginald's loyal subjects. He had faith that his brother would return safely, even though Reginald himself, who smiled and thanked everyone, had doubts about the outcome of the war.

Finally, Reginald and his men arrived at the convoy, where the king's mount awaited at the front. It was a beautiful white horse, adorned with golden tassels, a crimson saddle, and a golden bridle to match the king's armor. Once the last knight had mounted, Gabriel looked up at his older sibling sadly. "Chin up, Gabe," Reginald said with a smile. "I'll return soon, and we'll go trout fishing. You'll see." He began to turn away, then looked back at his brother. "Oh, by the way—a future king needs to know how to use a sword and lance. Your lessons start tomorrow. It won't be easy, so do me proud."

"I will, King Reggie!" Gabriel swore fervently.

"Very good," the king said, and winked. Then he snapped the reins, and the horse lifted its head and began to trot away. Reginald waved to his subjects one last time while Gabriel watched as his brother and the knights set off on their crusade, unsure if they would return.

The young prince closed his eyes and told himself, *I must have faith.* Then he waved once more and ran back inside the keep.

Reginald watched as his brother disappeared into the crowd, then turned back toward the path ahead, his head lowered in worry. *I must have faith*, he thought. Then, with a determined gleam in his eyes, he snapped the reins harder and went to war.

CHAPTER 1

LOSS AND GAIN

S even years.

After seven long, painful years of war and unrest, King Reginald's entourage was finally returning home for good. The war with Alamure had ground on at a low level for far too long, dragging more lives into it than it should have. Finally, both sides had called for a draw, and the king and his soldiers were returning home to their families, to a tiny kingdom of hope and peace. The entire realm was abuzz with excitement, but no one was more thrilled than Prince Gabriel, who had waited a very long time for this day to come.

As soon as he heard the news, Gabe bolted out of his room near the top of one of the northwest towers. As the wooden door swung open, slamming against the granite wall, he dashed at a dangerous speed down the cobblestone staircase, taking the steps two or three at a time. His hair fluttering around his ears, his bright blue eyes searched the large wooden portico across the keep as he hit the bottom step at a breakneck pace. The instant his feet touched the stones of the Great Hall, he sprinted toward the entryway, bursting into the bright sunlight a moment later. He skidded to a halt, raising a hand to shield his eyes from the sun.

All around the capital, the king's subjects were preparing for their ruler's return. Kitchens had opened early, so bakers and chefs could prepare a grand feast. Banners and tapestries adorned with the royal crest hung from every windowsill, window box, and oaken door frame. Joyous music played in the streets of the city, performed by musicians professional and amateur; and the townspeople danced as they sang of Reginald's triumphs.

The excitement made Gabriel even more exuberant. Being the king's brother meant that he would be the first to greet Reggie as his convoy passed through the town square. Grinning at the thought, Gabriel once again picked up his pace and sped through town, passing vendors, merchants, children, bakers, chefs, and many others along the way. It didn't take long for the prince to reach the middle of town, where hordes of people lined the walls of the wooden and stone buildings, awaiting their beloved king's return. They were mostly peasants, but a few were knights who had been tasked with staying behind and watching over the kingdom, should the attack hit the home-front.

Gabriel saluted them as he passed. Many were his tutors in swordsmanship and lance-work; all stood tall and proud in their glistening silver armor. Knights stood near each corner, still on guard, while others sat upon their destriers, maintaining crowd control should something dangerous occur. One of the knights finally noticed the prince, and motioned to the others to stand at attention, at which Gabriel nodded his acknowledgment and smiled.

The distant sound of fanfare, signaling the return of the troops, could be heard ringing through the valley. The knights and the king were on their way home, and were closer than he had thought! The prince's eyes widened with wonder as the sound of hooves echoed through the square. His grin grew as he clambered onto the grand fountain that sat in the middle of the square, in order to view the parade from a better angle.

As the thunder of hooves drew nearer, the townspeople fell silent and peered anxiously at the stone archway of the Halcyon Ridge Gate, waiting for the first knight to pass through the threshold. At the same time, however, Gabriel couldn't help but feel anxious. Ever since the war had

begun, he'd heard nothing but bad news: deaths, losses, food shortages...
A hint of worry set itself in the back of his mind, but he tried to push the
thought aside and focus on what was important at this very moment: seeing
his brother, the person he had grown closest to since their parents' death.

Just then, the first horse appeared with its rider, passing through the
granite arch; a white-and-brown splotched stallion. Upon the horse's saddle sat another silver-clad knight whom Gabriel recognized almost immediately, as the rider was his brother's close friend, and the knight's daughter was Gabriel's best friend; it was Sir Kameran Whitetail. The ivory
feather of his helm was easily recognized, for no other knight bore the
same color as he. His beard and mustache looked unkempt and his hazel
eyes unfocused, almost as if he were daydreaming or was in a trance. His
stoic gaze turned to the young man upon the fountain, and immediately
his expression changed to an odd mix of hurt, disappointment, and fear.
This look puzzled Gabriel greatly as he raised an eyebrow to Kameran,
who rode past without a word.

Not long after this strange exchange, the rest of the knights filed in,
two by two. Some had obvious physical injuries, bound in bleached lin-
en, while others seemed to have scars of a different nature, and others
showed signs of both physical and mental strain. None of them looked
satisfied with their victory. *What happened to them? Where is Reggie?* Gabriel
wondered, watching with a growing sense of confusion. He still hadn't
seen his brother, nor the steed he always rode: the pure white stallion
named Regnant, with the brilliant crimson saddle and golden bridle that
matched his rider's armor.

More and more knights filed in, but there was still no sign of Reginald. The fact that the king hadn't arrived first sent a murmur through the
crowd that worried Gabriel, although he had faith that Reginald would
be the last to enter through the cobblestone archway. However, steed after
troubled steed passed the fountain on which he stood, their riders seemingly unable to look at him, and still there was no sign of the king.

Fear began to eat at the pit of Gabriel's stomach. The townspeople
must have been worried as well, for louder murmurs began to erupt from

the crowd. The knights who stood guard seemed unaffected by the words and whispers, but Gabriel could see the glances of worry and unease that passed between them. One question was on everyone's mind: *Where is the king?*

The last mare passed through the archway, pulling behind her a wooden cart with a white cloth draped over it. Gabriel could only guess what was inside, and he swallowed the lump that formed in his throat. Then he jumped down from his perch to follow the cart. Many questions ran through his mind, questions that were probably racing through everyone else's as well. His shaking hand pressed into his stomach as he felt the knot there tighten, anxiety threatening to overwhelm him. He could see Sir Kameran leading the long line of soldiers toward the stables, where the knights would dismount and be taken in for healing and rest; but before he had a chance to speak with the Knight Captain, Gabriel felt himself being pushed in the other direction, back toward the castle's entrance hall.

He looked up to see his brother's chief adviser and his own tutor in statecraft, Lord David Whittenburg, ushering him inside. Whittenburg's expression seemed rather stoic, unfazed by the dramatic entrance of the returning knights. The two spoke not a word as Gabriel preceded the elderly scholar inside the keep. All his questions would be answered there, since there was soon to be a great feast for the knights and their king.

So he let himself be pushed through the front entrance as the large oaken doors swung shut behind him.

The news swept over the kingdom like a tornado: fast and furious, leaving no room for recovery. The king had gone missing upon the field of battle, and a thorough search had failed to find any trace of him. He was presumed dead, possibly felled by some sort of dark magic. His knights had relayed the message that night before their grand feast, and no one was more shocked than Gabriel. His brother was gone, probably dead...

The shock was too much for him. That night, he immediately ran to his room and locked himself inside.

That night he cried, more than any 17-year-old boy should have.

Once the announcement had been made to the entirety of Halcyon Ridge, people from across the land and beyond traveled to the castle to grieve and to convey their condolences to the young prince. Although he would have preferred to bury himself in his room for the rest of his life, Gabriel pushed himself to do the right thing. He sat in his brother's empty throne, thanking the people as they came, and accepting any gifts they had to offer to the family. David Whittenburg stood behind the grieving prince throughout the ordeal.

He couldn't have made it without Whittenburg and his two best friends: Caitlin Whitetail, the bubbly blonde sixteen-year-old whose father was the Knight Captain, and Arthur Darvoux, a fiery red-haired lad who was also seventeen, like Gabriel. His mother was the best seamstress in the kingdom, and made all of Gabriel's clothes. The two felt as though their friend would never recover from a loss as big as this, and didn't blame him at all for his dazed expression and withdrawn air. Not only had Gabriel lost the remainder of his family, but he had also lost a very important role model—and his personal hero.

Caitlin and Arthur were bickering over badminton in the castle courtyard one afternoon a week after the announcement, feeling awkward, when suddenly Caitlin stopped in her tracks and slumped. "This isn't the same without Gabe..." she muttered in a low, dispirited tone.

Arthur let the shuttlecock fall, and looked at her sadly. "You're right," he agreed. Simultaneously, the two of them looked up at a window high above. It was the window to Gabriel's room, and he was leaning out of it, peering down at them with the blank expression they'd seen on him so often lately.

Sighing, he brought his head in and turned away from the window, letting fresh air fill the room. Suddenly, there came a knock at his door. Gabriel rolled his eyes, annoyed. "It's not locked," he snapped. "Come in."

The door opened, and in stepped Lord Whittenburg, with several pieces of parchment in his hands. The man wore a tall wizard-like hat complete with white stars, a long robe that matched his headgear, and shiny black shoes. He had white hair that reached to the middle of his back, and a long white beard of the same nature. One might have mistaken him for Merlin if they didn't know better. He smiled gently to the young prince, who turned away from him and frowned hard. "What do you want?" Gabriel asked curtly, to which the old scholar simply sighed.

"Your Highness, there will be a... discussion in the dining hall tonight at dinner," Whittenburg started, adjusting the big round spectacles on his nose. "All those eligible to take the throne are asked to attend, and since you are next in the line of succession..."

He didn't get any farther, because Gabriel turned and glared at him. "What makes you think I can rule an entire kingdom?" he asked savagely. "I can barely decide what I want to wear every morning! I have none of the skills necessary for a king. I'm terrible with a sword, I can't make decisions, and I'm not even sure what a tax cut is!" He sighed heavily in frustration, crossing his arms across his chest like a child and turning away from Whittenburg, who only looked fondly at the youth. The adviser rummaged around in the royal wardrobe, found a short jacket for Gabriel to wear, and held it out to him.

"Sire, if I may say so, I do believe this is what your brother would want..."

Gabriel nearly growled as he whipped back around, his fists balled so tightly his knuckles had turned white. "How do you know what Reggie would want?" the young prince yelled. "You aren't his brother! You aren't his blood! Don't say such stupid things!" He turned back around as he had before, arms across his chest.

Lord Whittenburg was a bit taken aback by Gabriel's tone, but he nodded just the same, and looked down at the parchments in his hands. He decided not to push the issue. "You are quite right, Your Majesty," he said, at which Gabriel turned back and stared at him. "I am not King Reginald's brother, nor am I related to him in any way, so perhaps I would not know what he would want. All I was trying to say was this: think about your brother. What would *he* want for you?"

Gabriel continued to gaze upon Whittenburg in astonishment for a few moments, then put a hand on his chin in thought—so like his brother that Whittenburg couldn't help but smile. Finally, he sighed again, knowing the old man was right. "All right, I'll attend," he replied.

"Splendid!" Whittenburg lay the jacket across the bed for him. "Thank you, Sire, that is all I request of you," he said, turning around and leaving the room.

As the door closed with a loud thud, Gabriel looked at the jacket anxiously. Memories of parties and festivals spent with his brother came floating into his mind. He shook his head to clear his thoughts, then took the jacket and threw it over his shoulders before walking to and gazing into the nearest mirror to look himself over. He looked regal, and more like an adult every day—though he wasn't sure if that was a good thing or not. Sighing once again, he began to look for his boots. He needed to look the part if his brother really did want him to become king.

After washing up, he decided that he looked dignified enough and ready for a special occasion. Just as he reached for the doorknob, his two best friends burst in, nearly trampling the poor prince. "Gabriel!" they both yelled, looking around for him. The loud groan behind the door alerted them to his presence as he pushed away the door that had hit him, rubbing his head.

"I'm right here..." he said, as Caitlin enveloped him in a hug. He let out a grunt of pain, but he was pleased that his friends had come for a visit... even if they hadn't bothered to knock.

"Oh Gabriel! I'm so *happy* to see you!" Caitlin exclaimed, squeezing him tighter. Gabriel winced slightly, but smiled. He'd never been one to complain about getting hugged by a pretty girl.

Arthur joked, "You've been locked up in this room for so long, we thought you would never come out again."

Caitlin finally released Gabriel from her vise-like grip, and stepped back as he brushed himself off. "Nah, you can't get rid of me that easily," he replied, to which his friends grinned.

Caitlin then gave him a once-over kind of look. "Where are you headed, Gabe?"

"I'm off to have dinner with the rest of the people who think they can rule the kingdom," Gabriel said bitterly. He didn't want to think of who might be there, for there was one person in particular he was *not* looking forward to seeing.

Caitlin saw the disgust on his face and looked concerned. "Is there anything we can do to help?" she asked.

Gabriel smiled at her fondly. "Well, can you watch over the place while I'm gone? Someone might try to steal something while I'm not around." He winked.

The two friends stood at attention and saluted him. "Yes, Sire!" they said in unison. Then all three teens chuckled, and Gabriel tipped his non-existent crown before leaving them in his room.

The halls were empty as he trod through them. The clacking of his boots against the granite beneath his feet echoed loudly, making the place seem very lonely indeed. Gabriel was worried about this meeting, and about whom he might meet. There was one person in particular he didn't care to see, and that was his cousin, Prince Ayden Callisto of Holheim. Ayden was his mother's sister's son, and had other, more distant ties to the Halcyon Ridge royal family, but the two princes always butted heads whenever they met. They'd never gotten along, for Prince Ayden had frequently verbalized his disgust for Gabriel's brother being the king. This led to brutal brawls between the young men, resulting in one or both of them receiving black eyes, bloody noses, and more than a few scrapes and scratches.

Nor was he looking forward to meeting with the Elder Council, a group of advisers and family friends who aided the king in making his decisions. They were also in charge of the kingdom while the king was away, on business or otherwise. They weren't always the nicest people to deal with, especially now that Reginald was no longer in the picture, and Gabriel's stomach churned in annoyance as he thought of what those greedy old men and women would do. Would they give the kingship to him, or try to hold onto the power for themselves? Either way, it would be dangerous to get crosswise with them.

Gabriel shook his head slowly, trying not to think about his devious cousin and the arrogant Elder Council as he stopped in front of the dining hall, the large doors towering over him. Lord Whittenburg was standing outside, cordially greeting the guests as they filed in. He noticed that Gabriel had arrived on time and grinned from ear to ear. "Prince Gabriel, Your Highness!" he exclaimed excitedly, shaking the teen's hand, "thank you very much for coming. I must say, you look right dignified, Sire."

Gabriel took his hand from the adviser and smiled sheepishly. "Don't overdo it, David. I only came because you wouldn't leave me alone about it," The adviser chuckled, then directed Gabriel into the room. Loud voices boomed through the hall, and he saw that people were standing against or sitting down at the long wooden table, waiting for the meeting to commence. They all turned when they saw Gabriel enter, giving him a loud cheer. One burly man even shouted, "Hail Prince Gabriel!" and the others in the room followed suit. Gabriel's eyes widened; he was quite shocked. He peered around closely to see if his cousin and the members of the council had arrived yet. Not seeing them, Gabriel sighed and smiled, walking past the many who had already gathered.

Sir Kameran, Caitlin's father, saw him and bowed low in respect. "Greetings, Prince Gabriel. It's an honor to be here for you. Should you need me, I will assist you in any way I can." Gabriel smiled and thanked him, then continued to the head of the table, where his brother had once presided over meals. He put a hand on the arm of the wooden chair, and remembered the great adventures Reginald had told him about after he had returned from a journey or a battle.

Sighing, Gabriel sat in the chair and looked at the others. He could see that all the members of the council had just arrived, and were already scrutinizing the candidates for the throne. Their collective gaze fell upon Gabriel, and he could feel a shiver run down his spine. *What creepy people...* he thought.

Whittenburg let one more person through, then called for everyone to sit. The members of the council and candidates for the throne sat at the table, while the others stood behind them.

Gabriel looked around at the candidates. Seeing that he knew most of them, he began to believe that they were better people for the job than he was. Until, that is, he laid his eyes on the one person he was hoping wouldn't come but who, dreadfully, had: Prince Ayden. The two young men glared at each other from across the table, as Gabriel wondered what Ayden would have said about his brother. *Anything that comes out of his mouth will be rude, anyway*, Gabriel thought, and turned his attention to Whittenburg, who stood next to him.

"Thank you all for attending this dinner meeting," Whittenburg began. "We have an important matter to discuss: whether or not to appoint a new king to the throne. As you all know, our fair King Reginald was apparently lost in battle, but no body was recovered. This leaves us in a difficult position, and so, with the help of the Elder Council, I would like to propose that we decide, immediately, whether or not we should replace the king; and, if so, with whom."

Gabriel turned to look at the rest of the participants, who were staring at Whittenburg. Some were murmuring among themselves, including Ayden and his cronies, but Whittenburg spoke up once again and silenced additional chatter. "Now, for the first order of business: all those in favor of replacing the king, say 'aye'."

Ayes could be heard all over the room, and among those were Ayden and the members of the Council. Gabriel was surprised at the number of people who wanted to replace his brother. They must not have liked him as well as they let on. Gabriel looked up at his brother's former adviser, who winked at him. Something was going on, and Gabriel wasn't sure if it was good or bad. He simply sighed and let Whittenburg continue.

"All right, then, it is decided. We will have a new king," Whittenburg said, turning to the members of council. "Now the question is, who shall rule our kingdom?" Everyone looked at each other, unsure of what to say. Gabriel looked around, wondering who would be the first to speak up.

Just then, a young man with short, dirty blonde hair stood up and pointed to Gabriel. "Prince Gabriel is the old king's brother. He's the rightful heir!" he burst out. Gabriel's eyes widened, and suddenly, everyone began to murmur once more.

Ayden stood quickly and pointed angrily at his cousin. "He is not fit to rule! He isn't competent, and has no understanding of what needs to be done!" he shouted, at which every person in the room turned and glared.

"And I suppose ya think yer better for the job, eh, Prince Impatient?" called a crimson-haired lady from the crowd. She happened to be Arthur's mother, Madam Winter, her Scottish burr still evident in her voice. Ayden smirked at Gabriel, who was glaring at him furiously.

"As a matter of fact—"

"Right, then, no more bickering," Whittenburg barked, and everyone silenced themselves immediately, those standing sitting back down. He smiled to them all and started again, his attention and speech now aimed at the council members. "Now, as I see it, there are two clear candidates, both of whom are close relatives of the former king. Does everyone agree?" The elders murmured once more, then nodded to the adviser, who smiled. "Very well. Members of the Elder Council: all those in favor of Prince Ayden, say 'aye'."

The ensuing silence spoke volumes. Ayden looked around the room crossly and stood. "You wouldn't know a good king if he kicked you in the aft end!" he raged, then sat back down, pouting angrily and crossing his arms. Whittenburg grinned as he turned to Gabriel.

"All those in favor of Prince Gabriel's ascension to the throne?"

The thunder of "Ayes!" threatened to bring the ceiling down.

"Well, it looks like we have a new king. Prince Gabriel, will you rise for us, please?" Whittenburg asked.

Gabriel was stunned. He knew that he wasn't nearly the man his brother had been, and he felt ill-suited for the position, as he'd never been groomed for it—but he stood for everyone as requested. Cheers and many a "hear, hear" erupted from the crowd. Gabriel had never been cheered for as much as he heard then. He began to feel a bit overwhelmed. A blush crept across his face as he smiled sheepishly. Then, Whittenburg held Gabriel's arm in the air and called out, "Long live King Gabriel!"

Once it had been uttered, the entire room began to chant it. Gabriel looked up at his arm, then at Whittenburg, who beamed at him and let him go. "Welcome to office, King Gabriel. We will commence with your coronation ceremony in a month or so. Let's let this news sink in." Gabriel nodded and turned to the people, who were still chanting and praising him as their king. *Maybe I can do this*, he thought with a small smile.

Ayden was glowering at him angrily from across the room. The woman standing behind him with auburn locks simply shook her head with a slight smile as she watched her prince fume and fuss. Then Ayden stood up angrily and walked out of the room, the woman following close behind him.

Gabriel smiled broadly. All of a sudden, he'd gone from being a barely-noticed prince to the king of the land! He sat down in the king's chair, and thought back to the day that his brother had left for battle seven years ago. He closed his eyes and remembered what Reginald had said to him: "'If I don't come back, you are going to be the rightful king; remember that.' That's what he had said," the young king murmured to himself.

Just then, Lord Whittenburg clapped his hands loudly; everyone in the room looked at him and quieted themselves. "What are we waiting for, everyone? Let's eat! We have yet to dine on our fancy meal!" The room cheered once again, and the servants and cooks began bringing out food to the hungry people. Whittenburg sat next to Gabriel, smiling. "Well, King Gabriel, how does it feel to be in your brother's position?"

Gabriel looked at him, unsure of what to feel. He simply smiled a small smile and watched people eat. "Weird," he said at last, "but a good weird."

Whittenburg chuckled at this, and the two of them began to eat, chatting about his responsibilities and other topics. He had a new life and a new position, and he would have to learn everything about it, one way or another.

CHAPTER 2

A New Beginning

"**W**HAT?!?!"

Gabriel had finally returned to his room, where his two best friends were waiting for him. He told them about what had happened during dinner, and that he was now king of the realm. The reaction he had received was the one he'd been expecting; Caitlin and Arthur stared at him in shock and awe, their eyes wide. "They decided you're the king just now? Just like that?" Caitlin exclaimed.

Gabriel shook his head. "No, it was a unanimous vote by the Elder Council," Gabriel told her, "Although there was one person who wasn't too happy about it."

"I'll bet it was that no-good, arrogant cousin of yours, right? Ayden?" Arthur seethed angrily. He disliked the Prince of Holheim just as much as Gabriel did. His statement made Gabriel's grin broaden; then the thought of being king and having so much responsibility finally set in, and he felt overwhelmed once again.

"Guys, how am I going to be king?" he moaned. "I am *nothing* like Reggie!"

He turned to look through the window, at the crimson sunset filtering through the half-closed shutters. Shaking his head, Gabriel slowly walked over and pushed them wide open, peering out upon the scenery below. The town itself was full of hustle and bustle as they readied themselves for his coronation. Even this far in advance, arrangements had to be made, meals had to be planned, gifts and decorations had to be made or bought, and room and board had to be made available for all the guests who would be arriving to attend the momentous occasion. Sighing, Gabriel turned back from the excitement, looking at his friends, who were beaming at him. They had no idea…

As he returned to them, head hung in anxiety, Arthur put a reassuring arm around his shoulders. "Hey, don't worry so much, Gabe," he said confidently. "You may not be anything like your brother, but you're a lot of things that make you who you are, and that makes you special."

Caitlin nodded in agreement. "Yeah. You don't need to be like Reg- I mean, His Majesty Reginald, to be a great king, Gabe," she said, "You just have to do your best and be yourself."

Gabriel had to smile a little as his friends comforted him. He was thankful that they believed in him as much as they did. *Maybe I can do this,* he thought, and embraced his two best pals. "Thanks, guys," he replied.

"Anytime, buddy," Arthur responded with another grin.

"That's what friends are for, Gabe. Oh, I mean, King Gabriel," Caitlin replied, curtsying gracefully to him. Gabriel's small smile grew wider; his friends had faith in him wholeheartedly, their loyalty never faltering for a second. He then hugged the two of them again, more tightly this time. After a few seconds, he let go and watched his comrades leave. Afterward, he gathered himself up and undressed down to his undergarments, then crawled into his wood-framed bed and drifted into a deep sleep.

The next morning, he was awoken with a start by a loud *bang*. He rubbed his crusty eyes to find his best friends rummaging through his clothing. He leaned up out of bed, keeping his lower half covered, and frowned at them. "Hey! What are you guys doing?"

Caitlin and Arthur cringed as they heard his voice, exchanging a worried look. "Uh oh…" Caitlin began.

"Busted," Arthur finished.

They both turned to Gabriel with a sheepish grin. "Just what are you doing in my wardrobe?" he asked.

Caitlin blushed a little and turned away from him, since she'd noticed that he was in his undershorts. "I heard that you were going somewhere important, so..."

"We were looking for some clothes for you, so you look all dignified and whatnot," Arthur replied.

Gabriel shook his head and then stood up, walking to the closet. "Well, did you find anything good?" he asked.

"Yes!" said Caitlin excitedly. His friends pulled out a beautifully regal blue coat, edged with silver and gold thread, that reached to his knees. After that, Caitlin left the room out of respect, to let Gabriel get dressed fully. He threw on a white ruffled shirt and black trousers, and then took the coat and shifted it easily to his shoulders before looking at himself in the full-length mirror. He looked very much like a king should, he decided. Arthur hovered over his friend's shoulder as he called for Caitlin to come back into the room. As she entered, she gasped in excitement. "Wow! You look awesome!"

Arthur just put a thumb up and grinned with a wink. Gabriel had to smile at his friends. *So much confidence...* They then exchanged hugs, good lucks, and a few other words, and his friends left him. After that, Gabriel put on his adult façade, and exited the room with what he imagined was a royal gait.

As he turned and locked the door to his room, he heard the click echo around the stone hallway, which led to a spiraling staircase made entirely of gray cobblestone. The stairs went up into the highest room of the castle, though the tower itself wasn't the tallest in the palace. They also descended to the entrance hall, leading out into the grand courtyard and village square. Slowly he proceeded down the staircase, his mind filling with questions and concerns about the coronation, and about the month ahead of him. What would it reveal? How would he be as King? Could he do as well as Reggie? So many worries clouded his thoughts, and yet at the same time, he knew that there were plenty of people who believed in him, who didn't think he would fail in this endeavor. This thought made him smile, and he continued down the smoke-colored steps, the clacking of his boot-heels preceding him.

The clacking came to an end as he reached the last step, and his foot touched the brilliant crimson carpet of the entrance hall. Once there, he stopped and took a good look around the hall. Bright tapestries and banners hung along the walls, adorned with his family coat of arms: A gryphon rampant, black, against a backdrop of mountains argent and sky azure. Portraits of previous kings, all painted by local artists, also adorned the gray brick. Gabriel could see that a spot had been cleared, so that his brother's portrait could be placed there; it had been commissioned and completed years before, thank goodness. He felt his heart sink a little at the thought, but then he quickly continued on his way toward the throne room. David Whittenburg had asked to meet him there the day after he had been chosen. Remembering where he needed to be, he turned toward the grand wooden archway that led to the throne room.

The oaken entryway loomed high over his mahogany head, the timbers seeming to creak in the wind as a breeze blew by the future king. Memories of years past flooded his mind; fond ones of laughter and stories shared between himself and his brother, and many a trial that he had been allowed to attend. Nothing capital, of course; Reginald hadn't wanted him to be exposed to the seedier side of life, or the penalties that came from breaking the most important laws of the land. Perhaps he should have been, though, since his brother was no longer here…

Sighing heavily, he strode through the archway and into the room. The family crest and long, brightly decorated tassels and tapestries continued into this room as well, lining the walls, while the same grand red carpet flowed through to the back of the room, where a pair of tall golden and red thrones sat, empty but carefully cleaned and preserved, for use at any moment: his parents' originally, though the leftmost throne had been his brother's after the old king and queen had died. He came to a stop before the two gleaming structures, staring blankly at the place where his brother used to sit. Once again, he felt a small sense of discouragement as he stared at the golden throne, but he knew that he had to be strong and not let the past haunt him or cloud his judgment.

He heard the slow patter of more footsteps entering the room. He turned, and a sigh of relief escaped his lips as he saw his chief adviser walk through the doorway. Lord Whittenburg responded to Gabriel's sigh with a smile. "You seem most happy to see me, Sire," he said to the teenage monarch, whose sad expression expanded into a slight smirk.

"I'm just glad it's you and not my snot-nosed cousin," Gabriel remarked, to which Lord Whittenburg chuckled.

"No, Sire, Prince Ayden will not be joining us today," he replied. "Indeed, there are a few things I must discuss with you in private, Your Majesty."

This made Gabriel's smile fade into a half-annoyed, half-worried frown. "What kind of things...?" he asked tentatively.

The old scholar adjusted the silver-framed spectacles that rested upon his nose, then rustled the papers in his hands, reading carefully from one of them after clearing his throat."It seems," he began, "that the Elder Council has decided, through yet another unanimous vote, that you are to be put through a series of trials and tests to see if you are fit to rule. First will be a trial of good judgment, in which you will be tested on how well you make decisions; then a trial of battle skills, where your skills and judgment outside of the civil world will be brought to the test."

Gabriel's eye nearly popped wide out of their sockets, and his half-annoyed, half-worried look deepened. "Tests? I have to be tested before I can take the throne? David, I can't!"

Whittenburg simply gave him a confused glance. "Oh? And why is that? It is traditional. Your father and your brother did it, you know. Do you have so little faith in yourself, Your Highness?"

Gabriel turned away from him, his jaw and fists clenched tightly in frustration. Whittenburg saw this and cleared his throat once again. "My apologies, Sire... I didn't realize how sensitive a subject this was to you."

As he prepared to walk away, a sigh escaped Gabriel's mouth as he unclenched his teeth and hands, turning to the old man with an anxious expression. "No, it is I who should apologize, Lord Whittenburg," he said, at which the elderly scholar stopped short and turned back around, peering at Gabriel curiously. "I honestly don't have the skills that everyone expects me to have. I never expected to be king; nor did I want to be. I'm not my brother..." He turned away from the adviser as he said this, but the old man just shook his head at the young man's lack of confidence. Slowly he walked up to Gabriel and placed a gentle hand upon his back. Gabriel's head twirled back to Whittenburg directly, a surprised look in his eyes.

"You know, Prince- I mean, *King* Gabriel," Whittenburg began, "It's quite all right to be afraid of something, and it's brave to admit that you are frightened or nervous, and of what you are frightened. I appreciate that you told me. This way, I can better help you."

Upon hearing his adviser's understanding words, Gabriel finally managed to give Whittenburg a small, grateful smile. "Thank you," he replied. "I don't know where I would be without you."

This made the elder man chortle slightly. "Now *where* have I heard that before?" he said, partially to himself, placing his free hand upon his snowy-bearded chin in a thoughtful gesture.

"Did Reggie ever tell you about the things he was scared of?" Gabriel asked, taking a few steps toward the exit.

The elderly scholar made his way down the steps of the dais and joined him. "Oh, indeed he did. I don't think he would mind you knowing. Would you like to hear some?"

"Heck yeah!"

"First, there were the spiders, but honestly, who can blame him...?"

The two laughed and talked the entire length of the room about the things that the previous king had been worried or unsure about. Gabriel couldn't believe his ears. Some of the stories that Whittenburg told about his brother, the things that had worried or frightened Reginald, were the very same things that Gabriel himself was presently worrying over. It made him feel much better about his new role. A broad grin spread upon his face as they crossed the threshold from the throne room to the entrance hall, the gray stone walls echoing to the sound of their laughter. They stopped just outside the wooden archway, allowing their amusement to subside; then they turned their attention to the main door as a warm summer breeze blew through the hall once again, brushing their hair from their faces.

Gabriel's smile widened as he looked through the double doors. "Maybe I can do this," he said quietly, watching the sun as it rose over the mountaintops. The day was still young; there was still too much to do to prepare himself for the month ahead, and for the trials that he would have to go through in the interim. However, he now had the self-esteem and faith in both himself and his friends and colleagues to get through even the toughest battles, be they physical or within the confines of his own mind. Whittenburg saw this new look of determination upon his sunlit face and smiled broadly, before staring out into the morning sun as well.

"Your brother would be very proud of you, Your Majesty," he said aloud, which made the young man turn sharply to him.

"Good," Gabriel replied, "because I would like nothing more than make him, and my parents, proud of me." He then turned in the opposite direction and took off at his usual breakneck pace toward the dark cobblestone steps, racing toward his tower. A grin was plastered across his cheeks as he ran. This was going to be a good day, and he knew exactly what he was going to do first.

Whittenburg turned just in time to see the tails of his coat disappear into the distance, and immediately took off after him, crying, "Sire! Wait for me!"

Later that morning, Gabriel changed into more comfortable attire and met up with his best friends in the entrance hall. The trio slipped out of the castle gates before it became too crowded, and headed into town. When they arrived at the square, they could see that it was a lot quieter than it had been for the past two weeks. Some of the visitors had stayed behind to see the rest of what Halcyon Ridge had to offer, while others were involved in various chores and events to help prepare for Gabriel's coronation. There was a lot to be done: flour to be ground, recipes to be refined or mastered, cakes, pastries, and other desserts to be baked, food to be cooked, outfits to be tailored, and many, many decorations to be made and placed in and around the palace. Arthur, Gabriel, and Caitlin stared in amazement as they gazed upon the bakers, the sweet aroma of cookies, cakes, and other baked goods wafting out through the open windows. These were mostly practice dishes and the normal daily baked goods; the coronation versions wouldn't be prepared for weeks.

"This is amazing," Gabriel said, turning and smiling at his comrades. "I remember when they did this for Reggie's coronation."

"Remember what happened to the cake that year?" Arthur piped up, to which Caitlin and Gabriel both laughed.

"How could we forget?" Caitlin replied. "You tricked Whittenburg into thinking there was a dragon in the cake!"

Just then, Gabriel caught a flash of violet and gold out of the corner of his eye and turned toward the source: his cousin, Ayden, and Ayden's personal attendant, a red-haired woman in a flowing purple gown. Just seeing the two made his blood boil. What was worse, there was a young girl following close behind them, wearing servant's clothing and an iron collar around her thin neck. She was painfully thin, and her short blonde hair looked as though it had been cut by a child—or by a blind ape. Gabriel stared at her, heavyhearted. A slave... How could Ayden use such an innocent-looking girl as his slave? Or anyone, for that matter?

Caitlin and Arthur wondered what Gabriel was looking at and turned, seeing the girl. "Oh, no..." uttered Arthur.

"Poor girl," Caitlin added.

"That *bastard*..." Gabriel hissed menacingly under his breath as he continued to gaze upon the young girl. He shifted his weight to his right leg, and was about to stride toward his cousin to give him a piece of his mind. However, a hand came down on his shoulder and held him back.

When Gabriel looked back, he saw Arthur shaking his ginger head.

"Gabe, don't start any trouble. You don't need it."

Gabriel just sighed and turned back to his cousin, glaring angrily. Ayden was speaking to his attendant when the young girl turned and locked eyes with Gabriel. He gasped, and could only stare into her emerald eyes, transfixed. The girl stopped abruptly in her tracks as she stared. It was then that Gabriel knew he had to help the poor girl... although he didn't know what he could do for her. Although it was frowned upon, slavery wasn't expressly forbidden in his kingdom.

Yet.

Finally noticing that his slave hadn't followed him, Ayden turned around and strode back grumpily toward the girl, grabbing her hair in one hand. "Ashlyn! Pay attention, you stupid cow!" he cried. Ashlyn yelped in pain and cringed as he yelled at her. It was quite clear that she was afraid of her master, which enraged Gabriel even more. Thrusting her away from him, Ayden turned and strode away, as the two women followed. They continued down the street for half a block before entering an inn.

Gabriel never took his eyes off Ashlyn, a look of fury contorting his features.

"What a terrible thing to do!" cried Caitlin from Gabriel's right side.

"That guy deserves a good lashing!" Arthur exclaimed.

Gabriel shook his head and snapped out of his trance-like stare, staring at the ground with clenched fists. "I have to help her," he said to no one in particular, though the tone of his voice portrayed his unease.

His two friends smiled and nodded. "Agreed!" they proclaimed together, which made Gabriel smile a little and look at them.

"We'll need help, though," he replied, looking up toward the castle, the tall stony walls towering high over the square, "And I know exactly who to ask. Come on!" He took off back toward the castle, with Caitlin and Arthur hot on his heels.

CHAPTER 3

THE FIRST TRIAL

The sun shone brilliantly through the stained-glass windows of the castle's staircase as David Whittenburg walked slowly down the cobblestone steps, his head buried in his notes, adjusting his spectacles occasionally. Once he had reached the bottom step, he pulled himself away from his papers and looked around. For mid-morning, it was quiet in the castle. Normally lunch preparations would be taking place, and it would have been more crowded than ever. He smiled at the silence and continued on through the entrance hall toward the throne room, only to turn as he heard pounding footsteps approaching. Gabriel, Caitlin, and Arthur burst through the front door, breathless. He stopped walking to wait for them.

Gabriel saw Whittenburg and grinned. "David!" he called, screeching to a halt before the white-haired adviser. Caitlin and Arthur stopped beside Gabriel, all of them panting harshly and leaning on their knees to catch their breath.

"My, my, you three *are* in a hurry," he said to them. "What's the rush?"

"David, I need—"

Before he could finish, a group of men clad in silver armor clattered up and stopped beside Whittenburg. One of the guards leaned over and whispered in his ear, looking toward Gabriel as he did so. Gabriel tilted his head to the side and raised an eyebrow curiously. Once they were finished, the guards left to continue with their business, leaving all three teens with puzzled looks. Whittenburg looked at Gabriel with a confused gaze as well.

"Well, that was quicker than I expected. Your first trial is to start in an hour, Your Highness," he said, making Gabriel's eyes widen with worry.

"Already?! But... I'm not ready!" he exclaimed.

Whittenburg merely smiled to the three of them, shifting the papers around in his arms. "Caitlin and Arthur can get you ready, and I will meet you in the throne room. You are to prove you can be a just and fair king today."

"But David! I need your help with something!" Gabriel protested.

The old man shook his head and began to walk toward the throne room. "It will have to wait until after this," he replied, and waved as he walked away. Gabriel watched him leave, his expression one of exasperation and worry. He began ascending the staircase that led to his room, his best friends following him quickly.

"Well, *now* what are we going to do?" Caitlin asked. If Whittenburg couldn't help them, and Gabriel had to be in the throne room for his trial, then there wouldn't be time to help Ashlyn before nightfall. By then, it would be too dark, and the town square would be too well-guarded for them to sneak around. Arthur frowned hard as they walked. However, neither of them could even begin to imagine just what Gabriel was feeling. Worry clouded his mind, and his hands shook as he grasped the wooden stair railing.

Soon, the three of them reached Gabriel's room and slipped inside, closing the door behind them. Gabriel disrobed from the waist up, while Caitlin and Arthur searched through his clothing to find the best-looking shirt and jacket they could. While they searched, Gabriel stared through his open window at the mid-morning light shining brightly over the land. His land. He could see the entire town from his bedroom, and what a sight it was to wake up to every morning; that's why he'd chosen this room as his own. Resolute, he turned back to his friends. "We *will* help Ashlyn.

I know we will."

"How do we do that?" Arthur asked, picking up a shirt that was short and navy blue, with a semi-frilly collar.

"Yeah, it's not like we can go right up to Ayden and demand that he stop being mean to her," Caitlin chimed in, inspecting a fancy, long coat; a gold and red-colored one, with golden and ruby embellishments lining the seams. She smiled as she turned and waited for Arthur to slip the blue shirt over Gabriel's head. Once it was on, she turned him around and slid the regal coat over his shoulders, facing him toward herself and fastening the buttons on the front. "There," she said, satisfied with their work.

"No one can say you aren't king material now!" Arthur proclaimed.

Gabriel looked at himself in the mirror and combed his hair with his fingers, his short brown locks falling neatly around his ears. "I have to admit, you two have amazing taste."

"That's what friends are for," Caitlin replied.

"Thanks, you two."

"No problem, Gabe," Arthur said, grinning. "Now let's go to the throne room. You don't want to be late for your adoring public."

Gabriel rolled his eyes at his friends and left the room, followed by Arthur, then Caitlin, who locked the door behind her.

They strode down the same set of steps they had just ascended, and walked briskly toward the tall archway that led to the throne room. Gabriel had been in the room just that morning, and had suspected that he would soon be back again. *Well, here I am*, he thought as he walked up to the tall oaken doors, which were closed but not locked. Gabriel turned to look at the guards who stood nearby. Upon seeing him in his regal attire, they bowed low and pointed down another hallway to Gabriel's right. "Good day, Sire. The King's Entrance is through there," one of the guards stated, his silver armor making a lot of racket as he moved. "We were told to send you down to it as soon as we saw you."

Gabriel turned to look down the hallway toward which he had been directed. It was flooded with darkness; only a few lamps lit the wall, and a long burgundy carpet lined the floor, making the dark pathway seem even darker. He thanked the guard and turned to stride down this new hallway. It was one he had never been down before; the main door to the throne room had always been where Reginald and Gabriel had parted ways whenever he had been allowed to attend one of Reginald's audiences, so Gabriel had never walked the King's Entrance before that day. As he did, he could feel a chill running down his spine, and couldn't tell if it was from the cold dark hallway, or his own nerves getting the better of him.

As he peered farther down the hall, he could see someone standing near a curtained doorway, light flooding through the bottom of the cloth that hung from the frame. As he came closer, he could see that it was Lord Whittenburg, and sighed in relief. Whittenburg noticed Gabriel and his friends approaching and smiled grandly to him.

"I am glad you could make it," he said cheerfully to Gabriel, to which the youth merely shrugged and shot him a weak grin.

"I must please my subjects," he said.

"Indeed you must, and with fifteen minutes to spare. Now..." Whittenburg could see the worry in Gabriel's eyes and smiled at him gently, resting his wrinkled, parchment-weathered hand on the young man's shoulder. "I will be right here with you; should you need my assistance, just call me over," he stated in a reassuring tone. Whittenburg put a hand on the curtain, "Are you ready, Your Majesty?"

Gabriel nodded, and then entered through the curtain.

On the other side of the violet cloth, sunlight streaming in through the tall windows warmed the young man's skin. A fiery glow seemed to light up the audience as he looked around, his eyes adjusting to the brightness. He could see that many people had gathered to witness his first trial as king, and felt his hands beginning to shake as he started to get nervous. Then in the next moment, as all eyes turned to him, the crowd erupted in a sea of cheers and hails. A smile crossed his lips as he listened. Hearing them as confident in him as they were, his doubt dissipated a bit, and he was able to walk toward the thrones and wave to the people below. He was about to seat himself in the left-hand seat when he noticed Whittenburg out of the corner of his eye, shaking his head and pointing to the seat beside him.

The doubt and nerves returned as Gabriel gazed uneasily at his brother's throne. That was where his brother used to preside over matters such as these. It was still Reginald's.... But if Whittenburg said he had to, then he would get over his fear and take his rightful place in the king's seat. He walked to it and stood before the cheering townsfolk, raising his arms and forcing a smile onto his face as he scanned the crowd to see if his cousin would be there. He hoped he wasn't; but at the same time, he was praying that the servant girl Ashlyn wasn't in any danger. Not seeing either of them, Gabriel sighed happily. Then Whittenburg strode up beside him and addressed the crowd.

"Ladies and gentlemen! I present to you... The honorable King Gabriel!"

More hails rose from the already boisterous throng, but Gabriel didn't mind. He smiled as he watched them, happy for their excitement. Then two loud claps rose over the crowd noise, and the townsfolk quieted down quickly. Gabriel turned to Whittenburg, whose hands were clasped together, and waited for further action. Whittenburg smiled to Gabriel and nodded, which signaled to the young king that he could seat himself, which he did rather slowly.

Sitting on Reginald's throne... It wasn't an entirely new experience for him, as he'd occupied the seat in Reggie's place while receiving the condolences from his visitors after his brother's disappearance. But that had just been a temporary thing... or so he had thought at the time. He'd always imagined himself occupying this chair one day, but not under these circumstances. He barely heard what his adviser was saying to the crowd, and snapped out of his reverie just in time to hear him say, "Now, on with the trials. Please bring in the first case."

The broad oak doors swung open, and in strode a middle-aged man. He was dressed in peasant's clothing, wore a straw hat on his neck, and had rough blonde hair and dark brown eyes. Upon seeing the king, he bowed low to Gabriel, then walked to the side of the raised stage closest to Gabriel. Not long after the first man had entered, another middle-aged man, wearing the same attire as the first but in a darker color, with auburn locks and emerald-green eyes, strode in. As soon as he set his eyes upon Gabriel, he immediately dropped to one knee in respect, and moved to the opposite side of the stage from the first man.

Gabriel looked at the two men, chills beginning to creep back up his spine. Whittenburg smiled as the wooden doors shut behind two guards. "The trial is now in session! Mister Reid, please state your case."

The first man who had entered the room stepped forward, bowing once more to the king. "Your Grace; Your Highness. I am George Reid, a farmer of Brightfield. I am honored to be in your presence today. I am here to report a crime committed against my land and my family. This man," he then pointed to the other fellow, who scowled, "has been stealing food from my kitchen gardens at night, whilst my family and I sleep soundly in our beds."

The other man rolled his eyes and stared hard at Reid. Gabriel saw this look and turned to the first man. "Mr. Reid, how can you prove it was this man?"

Reid smiled respectfully at Gabriel. "Because, Your Highness, I caught him red-handed," he explained, his brow thunderous as he pleaded his case. "A few weeks ago, I noticed that certain things had gone missing from my garden while I was asleep, for they were no longer there when I awoke in the morn. So a few nights ago, I stayed up late to see if I could catch the thief, or animal if it had been one, and I caught this man sniffing around my carrots and cabbage." Reid pointed to the other man across the room, who had an arrogant air about him.

Gabriel noticed this and turned to him, though before he could speak, Whittenburg chimed in with, "Mister Charleston, you may state your case."

The second man, stepped forward as well and crossed his arms before him. "Yer Grace. Yer Highness, I am Henry Charleston. George Reid is addled, always has been. I didn't steal naught from him," Charleston proclaimed, but Gabriel wasn't convinced.

"Do you have any proof that you were not there, Mr. Charleston?" the young king asked. This made the second man lower his arms a bit, and give Gabriel a surprised look. Reid then raised a hand, and Gabriel nodded to him to speak.

"Sire! I have more proof that it *was* Mr. Charleston," he said, pulling a cloth from his back pocket to show to everyone. It looked to be a handkerchief made of purplish cloth. The audience gasped and murmured quietly as they all wondered aloud what would happen next. "I found this in my garden that same night I saw Henry there."

Charleston glared angrily at Reid. "How'd you get that? That's mine! I was never in your stupid garden!" The expression on Charleston's face portrayed a different story. Gabriel could feel his nerves aching again, and turned to Whittenburg, who leaned over so the two of them could speak quietly.

"What do I do?" Gabriel muttered. "I know who's right... Or who I believe is right."

To this, Whittenburg replied with, "I can speak for you if you would like, or you may pronounce the verdict yourself." He stood back up and raised his arms above his head, silencing the crowd. "The king has reached a verdict!"

He then turned to Gabriel, who tentatively stood and spoke with as much authority as he could muster. "The court finds Mr. Charleston guilty as charged with property theft. As it involves perishable goods, your sentence will be to repay Mr. Reid with hard labor. Work with him until the season ends, then your sentence will be up. And hopefully, you will learn not to steal from anyone again."

Charleston simply stared at the young king, his mouth agape, before sputtering, "Are... Is this... Are you sure, Sire?"

Gabriel nodded firmly. "That is my verdict, and your punishment."

"I-I was expecting something much worse... Thank you, Your Majesty."

"The punishment *will* be much worse if it happens again. Believe it."

Charleston bowed low to Gabriel. With the verdict cast, the two men bowed once again to the king and his adviser, and were escorted out of the throne room.

Gabriel sighed heavily and sat back in the seat, looking up at the old scholar. "That was easier than I thought," he said, relieved.

Whittenburg just smiled kindly. However, as he looked down at his docket, his smile faded quickly. "Oh dear..." he murmured, causing Gabriel to look at him curiously.

"What is it?"

Before Whittenburg could answer, the double doors swung open once more, and in walked the last person Gabriel had been expecting to see. His eyes widened, and he could feel butterflies in his stomach as he gazed upon the blonde slave girl. She had her head hung in shame, so seeing her face was next to impossible from where Gabriel was sitting, but he knew exactly who it was. "Ashlyn..." he whispered to himself, though Whittenburg heard him and gave him a puzzled look.

Ashlyn stepped forward and looked up, nearly jumping out of her skin as she gazed upon him. Gabriel stared back at her, and gave her a small smile. *I'll bet she didn't know who I was in the courtyard earlier,* he thought to himself. Then she stepped off to her right, where Charleston had previously been standing. Gabriel turned his attention toward the door once again, as the next person briskly and arrogantly walked toward him with a smirk on his mean little face. Gabriel had to stop himself from glaring furiously at his cousin as Ayden stepped up to him and nodded his head respectfully, though Gabriel knew that he didn't mean it. His cousin then stepped off to his left. Whittenburg must have noticed that Gabriel was looking a bit tense, so he cleared his throat and adjusted his glasses, then turned to Ayden and Ashlyn.

"Prince Ayden of Holheim, please state your case."

Ayden stepped forward and grinned. "Dearest cousin," he began in an oily voice, over-exaggerating every word, "I would like to bring to your attention the fact that this girl stole food from your pantry while my attendant and I were in the castle yesterday afternoon."

Gabriel's anger flared in his eyes, and many a thought ran through his mind, including bringing up the scene he had witnessed that morning between Ayden and Ashlyn; but he said nothing and turned his attention to Ashlyn, who hung her head in shame.

"What say you, young miss?" Whittenburg asked her sternly.

Ashlyn gripped her hands together and looked up at Gabriel, the faintest glistening of tears beginning to form on her eyelashes. "Please, Your Majesty..." she said, her voice light and airy, but shaky with fright, "I didn't steal the food. The lady in the kitchen let me have it. I was hungry, and I hadn't eaten all day."

Ayden gave her a deadly glare, as if he wholeheartedly refused to believe her. Gabriel turned to his cousin. "Why was Ashlyn hungry, Prince Ayden? Don't you take care of your..." Gabriel hesitated and firmed up his voice and he concluded, "...property?"

"She gets enough to eat," Ayden snapped, adding belatedly, "Your Highness."

"She may not agree. She seems rather thin. Can you prove that she stole the food, Ayden?"

Ayden's glare hardened. "Yes, I can." He snapped his fingers, and a woman Gabriel knew well walked in. It was the head cook, a short, stout lady with short black hair and beady brown eyes. She wore a powdery white apron, a long dress, and a mob cap, and had her sleeves rolled up. She curtsied to Gabriel, who nodded to her.

"Mrs. Fletcher," Gabriel said, "please give us your account of the events in question."

The cook bowed her head in respect. "Aye, Your Highness. I did indeed see the little miss sneaking into me kitchen yesterday afternoon," Mrs. Fletcher began.

Ayden let out a loud "Aha!", but Whittenburg shushed him and gestured to the woman to continue. "When I asked her what she was doing, she told me that her prince had been refusing to give her food because she wouldn't do exactly what he wanted her to do. I asked what those things were... and I won't repeat them here, Your Highness, beggin' Your Majesty's pardon." Anger flashed in her eyes. "Naturally, I couldn't let the girl go hungry, so I gave her a meal fit for, well, for you, Sire."

As Mrs. Fletcher finished, Ashlyn looked at her thankfully; she even smiled a little. Gabriel turned to his cousin, who was fuming.

"I do not starve her! She told you that lie so she could get free food!

She's a thief and a liar!" Ayden spat as he raised his balled fists. He looked as though he wanted to beat Ashlyn right then and there, but Whittenburg cleared his throat ominously, which silenced Ayden. Gabriel turned to his adviser, who walked over to him and leaned down so they could once again whisper.

"This is harder than the last one. I know he's my cousin and she's just a slave, but..."

"Your Highness, this is entirely up to you," the old scholar replied, "but if you would like my opinion, from the way Mrs. Fletcher told her side, the young lady's story sounds more promising. The food was not stolen, but freely given. And the girl does look painfully thin."

"I agree that Ashlyn didn't do anything wrong, " Gabriel answered in a low enough tone that only the two of them could hear, though his sneaky cousin was visibly straining to hear every word. "But what do we do about Ayden? How can we punish him for abusing his... his slave? More importantly, how can we make sure he doesn't do it again?"

This made Whittenburg smile, and he winked at Gabriel. "By your leave, I shall handle that, Your Highness."

At Gabriel's nod, Whittenburg stood and clapped twice to garner the audience's attention before addressing the two supplicants before them. "I have been given permission to speak for the King in this matter. Prince Ayden, we realize that you are a noble and have certain privileges that come from being born into that social class. But while you reside in our kingdom, however briefly, you must follow our laws. While it is clear that your servant girl did indeed enter the royal kitchens with the intention of stealing food from the pantry, she did so because of something *you* caused. Mrs. Fletcher is not pressing any charges, I assume?" He turned to the cook with a raised eyebrow.

The lady shook her head and said, "Indeed not, sir. She did nothing wrong."

"Well, then," Whittenburg said, looking to Ayden again. "The King does not appreciate those who waste his time bearing false witness against those who do not deserve such things. Do you not remember the sacred

Commandment? The penalties for breaking it can be... severe in Halcyon Ridge, Your Grace."

Ayden turned pale.

"But you are a noble, and so have some protection from the harshest penalties. Therefore," Lord Whittenburg continued, "the King has asked me merely to strip you of any authority you have over this young lady, Ashlyn, and allow her to come into the servitude of the crown. She is hereby manumitted, to become her own property, regardless of the original reasons for her chattel state."

The room erupted in whispers and murmurs once again, but Ayden's face turned redder than a ripe tomato in mid-summer. "What?! That's not fair! She's MY wench!" he shouted in embarrassment and anger.

This time Gabriel did stand up, his anger no longer containable as his fists clenched tightly. He glared at his cousin. "A servant is one thing, Ayden, but a slave is something completely different!"

Again the room was abuzz with wonder. They all fell silent as Ayden took a step forward, stabbing his finger at Gabriel; the guards at the door moved forward themselves, ready to step in and escort him away. "What are you talking about?" he hissed to Gabriel, who only glared harder.

"I saw you two this morning in the town square, calling her stupid and pulling her hair. Ayden, if this is how you treat all your servants, you might as well call them slaves, since they are not loyal to you by choice."

Ayden opened his mouth to retort, but nothing came out. His hand remained outstretched as though he wanted to say something, but he had nothing he *could* say; Gabriel had, after all, witnessed the whole scene that morning. While he was still standing and had the courage, Gabriel raised his arms and announced, "I hereby make my first Royal Decree, with God and you, my subjects, as my witnesses: From this point forward, chattel slavery is forbidden in Halcyon Ridge. Any slaves are to be immediately freed and provided with a means of income. Those who have none may work for the kingdom. Any traveler who brings a slave to this nation has the choice of leaving immediately or freeing that slave at the border. The penalty for flouting this law," he said sternly, "is death by execution.

No exceptions." He turned his smoldering gaze on Ayden, who shrank back, cowed.

The audience was dead silent. Even David Whittenburg had nothing to say.

The young king gestured at Ayden, and a guard took the erstwhile Prince by his shoulder and escorted him out. Meanwhile, Gabriel turned to the rest of the audience. "The rest of you may leave; that is all we have time for today," he stated. It wasn't a suggestion; it was a royal command, and they knew it. The crowd rose to their feet and began to file out, continuing to murmur and whisper to one another about the outcome of the trials.

Gabriel noticed Ashlyn leaving and scrambled down the stairs of the dais until he reached her, taking her arm in his hand gently. "Not you. I would like a word with you, if you please."

Ashlyn's face was aglow with a bright red blush as she looked at him, her eyes still very frightened. Gabriel smiled at her kindly. "It's nothing bad, I promise."

As everyone else continued to file out, Whittenburg walked down to the two of them and smiled gently. "Well, Your Majesty. You did very well indeed for your first time deliberating trials," he commented. He then smiled to Ashlyn, who returned a small, shy grin and looked at the two. "And you showed an unexpected gift for taking charge, with that first Royal Decree."

Gabriel smiled as he turned to Whittenburg. "Guess I did."

"By the way, Sire, with what did you need my help?"

Gabriel smile widened as he looked at Ashlyn, releasing her from his grip. "Nothing now."

Whittenburg gave him a puzzled look, but shrugged and said cheerfully, "Welcome, young lady. Ashlyn, I presume?" as he turned to the straw-haired girl. Ashlyn nodded, still not saying a word. Whittenburg bowed and took one on her hands in his. "You are very lucky, you know; for if you hadn't had Mrs. Fletcher to back up your story, you would likely be in prison." Her jade eyes widened, a slightly bewildered look in them. Whittenburg continued, "Now, what are you most skilled at?"

Ashlyn blushed even brighter and looked away from them both. "Um.... I-I can cook, clean..."

Gabriel shook his head. "What would you LIKE to do, Ashlyn?"

She turned to him, a little shocked. He had a feeling no one had ever asked her that question before. She looked at the ground, her eyes distant as she thought. "W-well.... I really like working with horses... Cleaning up after them, brushing them, training them. It's been a passion of mine since I was a little girl," she replied timidly, to which Whittenburg smiled and chuckled.

"Then it's settled. You will be our new stable lad," the elderly scholar said. "Or better said, stable hand, as you are not, in fact, a lad."

Ashlyn gave him the same surprised look as before, and then turned to Gabriel. "Y-You mean..."

Gabriel nodded. "Ayden doesn't own you anymore," he said gently. "No one owns anyone in Halcyon Ridge... and no one ever will again."

Ashlyn breathed a sigh of relief and smiled—a genuine smile that was happy, almost carefree. "Oh, I'm so happy... Thank you, thank you both!" she threw her arms around Whittenburg's neck.

"It was no trouble at all," Whittenburg said, adjusting his spectacles as she disengaged and embraced Gabriel, who was blushing himself now. He'd never gotten a hug from a girl before. Well, Caitlin... but this was different.

Lord Whittenburg stood and looked fondly at his king. "I'll show her the way, Your Majesty. Why don't you go meet your friends, and tell them the good news? I will also be having a word with the King of Holheim about his son's... misuse of his servants."

They left him in the throne room, Whittenburg chattering away about how much she would like working at the castle, Ashlyn looking up at him and listening with great care, focusing on every word. Gabriel just nodded to his mentor as they left. Then, once they were well gone and wouldn't see him, he took off at a dead run, a grin on his face. He had to tell Caitlin and Arthur what had happened, that Ashlyn was safe at last!

CHAPTER 4

A DAY OFF FOR GABRIEL

The entrance hall was nearly empty as Gabriel raced toward the tall structure that harbored his bedchamber, royal coattails trailing behind him. He had no thought for kingly dignity; he had to find his friends. He had so much to discuss with them. But just as he was about to set foot on the staircase, a hand came down on his shoulder and swung him around. His eyes widened in surprise as he came face-to-face with his rival.

Gabriel glared and pulled his shoulder free from the other boy's grasp. "How dare you manhandle me! What do you want, Ayden?" he snapped, standing a good few feet away from his cousin.

Ayden crossed his arms in front of him, his knuckles and fingers white from holding back his anger. "Your daft old counselor sent word to my father, and had my best servant taken away. I want her back right now!" he fumed.

Gabriel gave his cousin a puzzled look. The deed was done; there was nothing Gabriel would, or possibly could, do to change it. By tradition, no Royal Decree could be reversed for two years after its issuance without the unanimous approval of King and Council. He glared at the jealous boy. "Even if I could change it, I wouldn't," he declared. "After seeing the way you treated her this morning, I don't trust you with any of your own staff, let alone mine. Not to mention, you tried to put her in prison for stealing food that was freely given. And now you want her back? Why? To punish her yourself?"

The young king could almost see the steam rolling from Ayden's ears. His arms uncrossed and his hands balled into tight fists. He looked as though he was going to punch Gabriel, but just at that moment, a loud sound rang out from behind them. They both stopped and turned to the source of the noise. To Ayden's surprise and Gabriel's delight, it was Arthur, with a big grin upon his cheeks as he looked at Gabriel, clapping slowly.

"Ah, there you are, *Your Highness*," he said, exaggerating the last two words.

Ayden's face went a shade paler. A man could get executed for striking a king.

"Arthur! Just the man I was looking for," Gabriel replied. Arthur gave him a curious look that was followed by a shrug and a mischievous grin aimed at Ayden.

"So, Ayden, how does it feel to finally be put in your place?" the ginger-haired youth said, a touch arrogantly. Ayden simply scoffed, with his fists still balled, and stormed off toward the front gates. The other two teenage boys watched him leave as Arthur said loudly, "Gosh, I hope he doesn't burst into flame. The sun's still out, you know."

Gabriel laughed heartily to his friend's comment, to Ayden's obvious irritation. Once the Prince of Holheim was gone, the two friends embraced warmly. "So, you were looking for me?" Arthur asked as he pulled back, to which Gabriel nodded.

"I have something important to tell you and Caitlin. Where is she?" he asked hurriedly.

"Beats me," Arthur replied with a shrug, looking a trifle uneasy for some reason. "She's around here somewhere, though." Gabriel didn't wait for Arthur to ask why; he ran toward the castle entrance door, shedding his regal coat and handing it off to a maid. He nodded and thanked her as she smiled, then took off through the very same portal his cousin had exited not a few moments prior. Though he still looked rather confused, Arthur rapidly followed the young king.

The warm sunshine soaked into their skin as their gait slowed to a fast walk. Once outside the large stone entryway, the boys could see the bustle of the town square in the distance. They hurried toward it; the square was easily one of Gabriel's favorite places in the kingdom. With a smile on his face and a twinkle in his eye, he scanned the stalls and vendors, looking for his other best friend. Finally, he spotted her bouncy blonde locks among a crowd of dancing girls, all of whom were older than the three of them. When the ladies spotted the boys walking toward them, they began to giggle and chatter amongst themselves, like songbirds on a sunny day. Caitlin wasn't among these girls; she had pulled herself away from the group to turn to her friends with a pleasant smile.

Gabe noticed that Arthur was returning her smile with a silly grin of his own, his cheeks a bit red. He ignored that as Caitlin cried, "Hi, Gabe!" Then she remembered to curtsy and bow. "Oh! I mean, good day, Your Highness." The group of girls snickered and giggled even more, echoing her comment and curtsy, which made Gabriel's own cheeks flush.

"Caitlin... You don't have to do that..." he whispered slightly as he looked away.

Arthur just laughed at the two. "So, Gabe, what's this big news that you have for us?" he asked, to which Caitlin looked up at Gabriel with a puzzled expression.

"Big news?" she parroted.

Gabriel looked between the two of them and grinned, taking their hands and leading them back toward the keep. "There's something I want to show you," was all he said, and then the trio walked briskly toward the castle's stables.

The courtyard of the castle was quite busy, with servants and other people of importance rushing about, not only preparing for their new king's coronation but carrying out their normal duties as well. However, before the three friends reached the castle gates, they took a sharp turn down a dirt path toward the stables. Caitlin and Arthur were giving Gabriel and each other confused looks, wondering where their comrade was taking them and why, but he said not a word as he led them on. Soon the rich smells of hay, sawdust, manure, and horses filled their nostrils as their neared the stables. A loud clanking sound echoed from a small building off to their right. As the trio slowed to a brisk walk, they peered inside the small building and saw a large arsenal of armor, metal plates, and colorful bridles and saddles. The armor shone brightly from the polishing it had recently received, and they could see many people working hard to get the equipment ready for the big day, adding tassels and other decorations to the saddles and such.

Gabriel kept walking, his eyes scanning the barn's exterior. He was determined to find her. Arthur and Caitlin were right behind him, looking around at the decorations and preparations being made. Inside the barn, the busyness increased tenfold, and it was causing the horses to become edgy and skittish. Some shied away from their handlers, while others whinnied and bucked wildly, obviously agitated by the swiftness of the servants' movements. Just then, there was a loud clattering of hooves and a few shouts as one of the horses pulled loose from a stable lad. It raced toward the open barn door, right where the trio was standing. Arthur and Caitlin gasped in shock and dove out of the way quickly, but Gabriel's eyes narrowed as he rushed toward the frightened animal. His friends were even more surprised, and it showed on their faces.

"Gabe!"

"Hey, come back!"

Gabriel wasn't frightened. As soon as the horse saw him, it stopped abruptly and reared, its front legs raised and kicking in the air. Gabriel could see that the horse's lead rope was long enough for him to grab, and he did so carefully, gently pulling on it. The horse jerked its head away from Gabriel, but as the king held onto the rope, someone slipped between him and the horse, pulling its head down to eye level.

"Hey, whoa, whoa, Aztec! Easy there, boy..." the stable hand said softly and gently, patting the tuft of mane between the horse's ears. As if by magic, the horse calmed. He sniffed and whinnied one more time before lowering his head and standing peacefully before the girl in the stable lad's cap, calm as an undisturbed lake. Caitlin, Arthur, and Gabriel, as well as the rest of the stable staff, stared in awe at the scene. A horse gone crazy, settled down by a slip of a girl; it was unheard of. Even as everyone else stared, Gabriel grinned and put a hand on his hip, handing the lead rope back to the girl, who had yet to reveal herself.

But Gabriel knew who it was. "Thanks, Ashlyn," he said loudly. Another gasp echoed from behind him as the girl took off her cap, her bright hair shining, and turned toward the king, her face red as she took Aztec's lead rope. "Oh, uh.... Y-Your Highness! I, I didn't see you there!" she stuttered in embarrassment, looking down at the floor, "...I apologize for Aztec's behavior... He's just nervous and antsy from all the activity."

"No need to apologize, Ashlyn," he replied, "you did well." Her cheeks reddened even further, and she smiled shyly and turned away to look at the horse beside her. The previously wild beast was munching happily on some hay on the dirt floor of the stable. Just then, Caitlin and Arthur snapped out of their daze and stepped up beside Gabriel, smiling at Ashlyn.

"That was so cool, Ashlyn!" Caitlin said softly, so as not to scare the horses.

"Simply amazing," Arthur agreed.

"Couldn't have said it better myself, kids," came a voice from behind the three of them. They swiveled around as the sound of armor echoed through the barn. Caitlin grinned widely and ran toward the metal-clad man.

"Dad!" she exclaimed as she embraced him tightly. The man smiled as he looked at her, then at the other young people before him. Arthur bowed in respect, while Gabriel simply lowered his head.

"Sir Kameran," he said, as Kameran smiled back.

"Good to see you, Sire," the Knight Captain replied, turning toward Ashlyn. "Thank you for calming him, miss. I know he can be stubborn sometimes." He knelt to give his daughter a hug and a kiss on the cheek.

Then he strode over to his horse and took the lead rope from Ashlyn, leading the horse down the long length of the barn toward his stall. Ashlyn fiddled with the hem of her shirt timidly—she was now dressed in the traditional stable lad's simple tunic and trousers—as she watched Sir Kameran leave. Caitlin returned to her friends, looking over at the young girl.

Gabriel quickly introduced her to Arthur and Caitlin. "So, if you're here, Ashlyn, where is Ayden?" she asked. Ashlyn looked away as her blush faded into a look of sadness. Caitlin saw this, and quickly covered her mouth in embarrassment, while Gabriel stepped forward, standing beside the girl.

"My cousin is no longer Ashlyn's master, thanks to Whittenburg and me," he said.

Arthur grinned. "Hah! I knew he would get his just desserts!"

"How did you do it?" Caitlin asked.

Gabriel smiled proudly. "Made my first Royal Decree," he boasted, and then proceeded to tell them about his exploits in the throne room. The stable hands stopped to listen in. Everyone was so enthralled by his tale that once he had finished, they seemed reluctant to go back to work. Soon, however, everyone had returned to their duties as before—everyone except Ashlyn, for Gabriel was still talking to her along with his friends.

"Wow...." Caitlin and Arthur murmured when he had finished. Gabriel smiled broadly as he turned to Ashlyn, who blushed slightly and looked at the ground with a tentative smile.

"Yeah, it was pretty great."

A stable worker called to Ashlyn just then to help with a skittish horse, causing all four teens to turn. Gabriel smiled and patted Ashlyn on the back gently, and said, "Go ahead, Ash, we'll catch up with you later." She quickly turned to him with flushed cheeks, but then she smiled sweetly and nodded, running off to help with the beast. "Thank you, Sire!" she shouted back to him. Gabriel watched her go, a satisfied look in his eyes, while the other two grabbed him by the hand and pulled him away from the scene. Caitlin and Arthur looking at each other meaningfully as they dragged him away, and finally managed to get him outside again and walking toward the castle. This time Gabriel didn't know where he was going, but had a feeling he would soon find out.

Once they were on their way back toward the entrance to the castle, they could see that the courtyard had indeed become very busy. Many vendors and chefs and various staff members were bustling about, tending to their business. The gardeners worked overtime with the gardens and hedges of the front yard, shaping them toward perfection for the king's special day. Gabriel smiled as he watched all the hard workers, knowing he had wonderful people helping him and taking care of the castle. He admired them—though Caitlin and Arthur continued to pull him inside, so he admired them from a distance.

As the companions ushered their royal friend in through the front door of the castle, Gabriel could see that the entrance hall had become extremely crowded in a short time. There were now many more people populating it than when he had left earlier that morning with Arthur. The trio looked at the throng of people nervously. Were they all here to see Gabriel? Most of them looked aristocratic and important. He also spied a few young girls who looked to be about his age; Arthur had spotted them too, grinning and nudging his friend's arm playfully.

"Hey," he said in a sly tone, "What do you think of them, huh? Those girls are pretty cute, aren't they?" Gabriel only turned to him and gave him a strange, puzzled glance, while Caitlin glared at him, then smacked the palm of her hand against her forehead.

"Oh boy..." was all she replied with.

"Oh... um, sorry?" replied Arthur, his face flushed as he withered under her stare. Gabriel shook his head, considering the crowd again. It was then that he saw his counselor walking among the people. As he spied the three of them, Lord Whittenburg smiled and pushed his way through the crowd toward Gabriel. Once he had finally freed himself, he stepped to Gabriel's side, adjusting his spectacles once again.

"Sire! There you are, I have been looking for you everywhere," he said, to which Gabriel turned his surprised glance toward him, his eyebrows raised.

"You have? What for? What's wrong, David?" Gabriel asked suspiciously, unsure of what was going on.

"Your next test will start tomorrow morning, bright and early, when you are needed in the summit room, Sire. Please make sure that you are ready by then."

Gabriel only gave his adviser a small nod, leaning to the left to gaze upon the crowd behind him. "All right—though I do have one question," he said tentatively, to which the elderly scholar gave him a strange glance. "What's with all of the people in the fancy clothing?"

Puzzled, Whittenburg turned his gaze to where the young man was pointing, and laughed as he turned back to Gabriel. "All of these people are here for an audience with the new king," he explained. "Most of them are here for the coronation, or to speak to you about important matters, and yet others are awaiting your presence, merely to see you, whether it be to give you condolences or to give you gifts."

Gabriel looked from Whittenburg to the crowd, nervous about the amount of attention he had somehow attracted to himself. It made him a little uneasy, but he figured that it came with the territory; after all, being king wasn't going to be easy. At that moment, a group of soldiers walked up to them, bowing as they noticed Gabriel. Then one of them turned to Whittenburg and whispered low, so that only the counselor could hear. This puzzled the three friends, as they all tilted their heads to the side in curiosity. "What are they talking about?" Caitlin asked, to which the boys simply shrugged in confusion.

"Beats me," responded Arthur as he watched the older gentlemen. Soon, the men finished their conversation and went their separate ways, bowing to each other once again. Whittenburg adjusted his spectacles once more and peered at the parcels in his arms.

"Well, that was unexpected," he said to no one in particular, then his gaze returned to the three companions with a cheery smile. "Well, Sire, it looks like your trial has been moved to tomorrow afternoon instead, so you are free to spend the rest of today and tomorrow morning as you wish." The three friends then cheered in delight, their voices resonating about the castle walls, making everyone's heads turn. Whittenburg chuckled at their enthusiasm, a look of relief in his own tired brown eyes. Gabriel then turned to his counselor with a curious gaze.

"But then..." he asked, "What am I supposed to do all day?"

Arthur put his arm around his companion's shoulders playfully, a wide grin across his face. "I know exactly what we can do, Gabe," he replied, his eyes averted to the throng of individuals standing near the throne room entrance. They had all turned away from the young king, murmuring and whispering quietly amongst themselves. Gabriel turned his attention toward the crowd of royals; many of them were older, parents or rulers of small kingdoms, while others were young adults, most of whom were his age. In fact, they all seemed to be young ladies dressed head to toe in fancy gowns and impractical shoes, their hair was done up in tight buns or high ponytails. He peered at these young ladies curiously, then at Arthur.

"You really think you'll find someone for you in there?" He laughed out his answer. "They probably wouldn't look twice at you, as snobby as they are!"

Arthur glanced at Caitlin and laughed heartily, which confused the young king immensely, his eyebrow raising in puzzlement once more. "I'm not talking about me, Gabe!" Arthur chortled. "Those girls are here to see YOU!"

Even Caitlin started to laugh, as the two friends watched Gabriel's astonished reaction. "Wait, what?"

"Wake up and smell the bread baking. They're here for *you*, Gabe," Arthur explained. "They want to marry you. Duh."

Gabriel's eyes widened farther as he stared at his friend. "But..." he began, then tried again. "But why do I have to get married? Reggie never got married!" His voice was a bit louder than he'd intended it to be, reverberating off the stony walls and ceiling. Everyone turned to stare at him, and his cheeks flushed as he felt everyone's eyes upon him once again.

His friends giggled at his embarrassment, but Whittenburg merely smiled gently. "Well, Sire, it *is* important to wed fairly soon and provide an heir, just in case something should happen to you. For example, if someone should attempt to take your life…"

Gabriel whipped his head back to look at his adviser. "Who would want to kill me?" he asked flatly. His friends shrugged, but Whittenburg bowed his head thoughtfully.

"That I do not know, Sire, but remember what precipitated the war that ended in Good King Reginald's loss. Please keep an open mind, Your Majesty."

With that, he bowed and walked away into the crowded hall.

Gabriel stared at him as he left, then at the people before him. He was feeling very unsure about the pressure that had been forced upon him, and he bit his lower lip nervously, something he hadn't done since his brother's mysterious disappearance. He began to think about this marriage…. Did the lucky lady have to be royal? What if they hated each other? What if she smelled bad, or had an unsightly mole on the back of her neck, or…? Many such thoughts raced through his troubled mind.

He felt two arms draped over his shoulders. "Don't sweat it, Gabe!" Arthur said.

"Yeah," Caitlin agreed, "We've got your back. We won't let you marry a snobby little witch who only wants you for your title." Their confidence was enough to make Gabriel smile, and he returned their embrace warmly.

"You guys are the best," he said, and the friends laughed together and talked about how they were going to spend the rest of the day.

CHAPTER 5

LADIES, LADIES, PLEASE!

Later that night, as Gabriel was readying himself for bed, he continued to think about the day that lay ahead. He wondered about the trial in the war room, what was to be expected of him, and what kind of decisions he would have to make. He felt a little intimidated by that, for he had no idea who, or what, would be there. They would be watching him closely, waiting for him to make a mistake or for him to falter, even just once. He knew he had to do his best, but at the moment, he felt his best might not be enough.

He was also thinking about what Whittenburg had said that day about getting married, something he was very much *not* looking forward to considering. Annoyed, he thought about how he might determine with whom he would spend the rest of his life, ruling together as king and queen. He had no idea how to speak to women the way a courting man would, or even how to get their attention. He decided that he would ask around the next day; he would talk to married couples and ask them about how they'd first met, if they were in love with each other, what they loved, what they hated, things that pertained to being in a long-term relationship with someone. Asking around was always the best way to find out information, or so he'd always found. Smiling at the thought, he put his mind at ease and undressed down to his undergarments, then pulled the covers back on the warm four-poster bed and crawled under the covers, snuggling in and falling into a deep, undisturbed sleep.

The next morning, the sun filtered in through shuttered windows as the sun rose, making lines of shadow and light along the floor that reached to the door. One ray of sunshine crept its warmth across Gabriel's serene face, and his eyes fluttered open slowly, his hands reaching up to rub the sleep from his heavy eyes. He yawned loudly and leaned himself upward toward the ceiling, much like a cat awakening from a nap, as he stretched his arms and legs outward away from his body. He then turned his attention to the half-open shutters, and smiled sleepily, swinging his legs over the side of his bed, letting his feet dangle above the floor.

"Today is going to be a good day," he announced to himself, hopping out of the comfy sheets and onto the warm hardwood floor. He then walked to the window and threw the shutters open, allowing the sun to illuminate the rest of his bedroom. He could feel the heat on his skin, bringing a smile to his lips as he looked out upon the town square and castle courtyard below him.

Early morning wouldn't normally be too busy; farmers, ranchers, and stable hands would begin their day by tending to their animals, while about the courtyard and entrance to the town, the night guards would be replaced with well-rested day-time knights, armor shiny and polished. A few of the castle's pets would still be lurking about the courtyard and gardens, looking for an early morning snack or two, rousting out pests as they did, while the bakers and chefs would begin to bake and cook breakfast for the entirety of the palace. Gabriel always enjoyed the smell the freshly baked breads and meats as the aromas wafted up to his room.

However, that morning was busier than most; the town square was bustling as shopkeepers, florists, and other vendors opened up shop, preening and preparing their merchandise for an early morning rush of customers, which was to be expected due to so many visitors in town. The inns were near to bursting with travelers, as were the castle's guest chambers. In the courtyard directly below Gabriel, gardeners trimmed and tended to the gardens of fresh vegetables, flowers, and the lush green hedges that lined the castle walls. Other servants and workers had started their work earlier, sweeping the cobblestone path that led toward the town square and dusting the main gate. The young king could hear the sounds of metal banging and clinking from the stables as some of the horses had their shoes replaced, and from the town below, where blacksmiths were forging weapons and other metal trinkets. Yes, it was definitely busier than usual in the kingdom that morning.

Gabriel turned away from the window and the busy world below his bed chamber, leaving the wooden shutters open to light up the room. He strode over to his towering wardrobe and threw open the oaken doors, peering into the mess that was his clothing. He needed to dress the part if he was to, as Arthur so eloquently put it, 'impress the ladies.' At this thought, Gabriel shook his head, then proceeded to choose his outfit. He began with a light-brown vest made of a soft leather that would be easy to move around in. Then he pulled out a forest-green shirt to go with the vest, as well as a pair of gray slacks, and of course clean undergarments. He'd taken a bath the night before; he'd never been one of those once-a-week-whether-he-needed-it-or-not fellows. Satisfied with his choices, he brought all these to the edge of his bed and began to lay them out neatly. He then proceeded to dress himself with each item, one by one.

There was supposed to be someone to help him dress, but he figured if he couldn't dress himself, he shouldn't be king. Not that he was especially private in that regard, but he'd been used to doing for himself since he was quite young. When Gabriel and Reginald's parents had perished suddenly, both the boys had been devastated. Though Reginald had recovered his sunny disposition fairly quickly, Gabriel had become re-bellious, insisting on doing most everything on his own. His independence often got him into trouble with the servants and Elder Council, who would scold him severely, especially when his brother was away on business or war. However, the final punishment, if any, was always left up to Reginald, who was a lot kinder to his brother than some siblings were to theirs. Usually the punishment was to work with the person he had wronged, whether it be washing dishes for the cooks he'd stolen food from, working in the gardens for trampling them to pieces, or helping in the stables for scaring the horses. Gabriel never minded the work; it kept his mind off other thoughts that were none-too-pleasant.

He became misty-eyed as he remembered those days. His heart began to ache for his idol, his older brother, wishing that *he* could be there to watch Gabriel rise to power, or better yet, to retain that power and go on to continue his interrupted rule. Gabriel knew that Reginald wasn't going to be coming back, so he had to face facts... Although, deep down inside, he had an odd feeling that his elder sibling was still alive, and that he would return to their fair kingdom, to rule as king once more.

What a stupid idea, Gabriel berated himself as he quickly wiped a tear with a dark-green sleeve, and finally finished clothing himself. He pulled on his stockings and his black, calf-high boots, tugging on the laces and tying them into a neat little knot. He then turned and looked at himself in the tall reflective glass against the wall, admiring his appearance. He looked much older, and more like an adult each passing day—so much so that it was beginning to frighten him. Shaking his head to clear it, he adjusted his vest and hair a little, then turned around and hurried to the door, exiting his room quickly.

As he closed the door behind him, he heard a chuckle, and whipped around quickly to see Arthur leaning against the gray stone wall of the tower stairs. His friend was dressed in an outfit like Gabriel's, but his shirt was white instead of green, and his leather vest was a darker brown. His long pants were black, and he sported brown shoes instead of the boots that Gabriel wore. His neat orange locks were swept back, and his brilliant green eyes shone with excitement.

"Wow, Gabe," Arthur said in half-surprise, half-amusement, "You really clean up nicely. And you didn't even need any help from me and Cait."

"I *can* dress to impress, you know," Gabriel retorted with a smirk.

Arthur just shook his head and pushed himself away from the wall. "Ready to meet the love of your life?"

"No," Gabriel replied simply, which made them both laugh out loud.

They turned away from Gabriel's room and began their descent toward the Great Hall, where a crowd of girls and parents would be waiting for them. As they walked, Gabriel couldn't help but wonder about the girls and what he would learn. The same worries he'd been entertaining about the previous day returned to his mind, making a knot form in the pit of his stomach. He subconsciously placed his hand upon his abdomen, trying to quell the butterflies before they saw the ladies, but to no avail.

Arthur saw nervousness and nudged him gently. "C'mon, stop worrying so much," he said. "You'll do fine."

"I don't see *you* angling for a bride," Gabriel retorted.

Arthur blinked and replied. "Well, um. I. Well. I'm, uh, beginning to think I don't want to. Or, really, I don't need to…" he trailed off, sounding flustered and uncertain.

"Going into the priesthood, then?"

"Argh, no! They'd make me shave off some of my hair! Could you imagine me with a tonsure, like Sir Calvin's giant bald spot?"

This made Gabriel smile a little, and the two continued down the stairs in silence… and it occurred to Gabriel as they approached the Great Hall to wonder what Arthur had meant by saying he 'Didn't need to' look for a wife.

As the boys reached the last granite step, they saw that the entrance hall was filled with the same crowd from yesterday. The butterflies in Gabriel's stomach worsened as he lay his eyes upon all the girls, all dressed in their best and powdered and rouged to perfection, not a plain or dumpy one in the bunch. His companion gave him a nudge once again as well as a wink.

"Just you watch this," he said playfully, and before Gabriel could retort, Arthur had walked toward the girls and bowed low. "Greetings, lovely ladies and parents! I present to you the honorable, and very handsome, King Gabriel!" The parents clapped and cheered, while the young ladies tittered and smiled, as if overly excited to see him. Gabriel could feel his cheeks growing hot with embarrassment as he looked upon them. Arthur's enthusiastic announcement had caused an uproar of excitement and jubilation from these people, all of whom apparently supported him in his rise to power. This only made him smile more, but he then heard his redheaded friend continuing with his speech.

"Now," Arthur said authoritatively, "We will begin the process of deciding who shall become King Gabriel's bride by a single test." To this, Gabriel raised an unsure eyebrow, as murmurs of curiosity and annoyance arose from the crowd before them. *What is it with these people and their tests...?* Gabriel thought, as his friend continued yet again, "And this test shall be a dancing competition! So ladies, grab your best dancing shoes, and follow us to the ballroom!"

Arthur turned to the young prince with a teasing wink, and then took Gabriel by the arm and began to lead him and the parade of young ladies behind them toward the ballroom. Gabriel didn't understand how dancing would determine the best bride for him, but he simply shrugged his shoulders and followed his friend. "I'm in for a long day, aren't I?" he asked, slightly exasperated.

"The day has only just begun!" Arthur replied, putting a reassuring arm around Gabriel's shoulders, "There are many, many ladies to choose from. One of them is bound to become your wife! This little test I've concocted will help weed out the ones who aren't a good match for you."

This made Gabriel smile a little, and he looked back at the young ladies as he walked. Would he really be able to find the girl he would call his wife in this group of noble girls? Well, there was one way to find out.

The ballroom was located right next to the throne room, but it was much grander; when it was empty, a single person's voice could rebound off the off-white stone walls and carry all the way to the dazzlingly high ceiling, which was elaborately decorated with pillars and gargoyles of marble, and chandeliers of tinted glass. The royal crest adorned the many tapestries and banners that hung along the ivory walls, creating an elegant atmosphere. The freshly waxed cherry-wood floor of the ballroom ended at the door frame, which was also made of a beautifully polished cherry.

Arthur and Gabriel peered inside slowly and carefully, looking all around to make sure the coast was clear. Arthur grinned as he spotted the band preparing to practice a few musical numbers. Swiftly he made his way toward the musicians, speaking with them quietly. Gabriel walked slowly into the room, staring up at the high ceiling and spinning in a circle, taking in the refined look of the room. Memories of past parties and grand balls floated gently into his mind, visions of older ladies and gentlemen dancing gracefully about this very same floor, twisting and twirling effortlessly to the rhythm of the band's melodies. It made him smile as he remembered.

Just as quickly, those memories faded, and Gabriel shook himself back into reality as the ladies who had come to see him filtered into the room. The girls looked rather confused, while their parents seemed irritated, judging from the way they were tapping their feet against the floor and the way their arms were crossed over their chests. Gabriel hurried over to Arthur, who had finished chatting with the musicians, and looked at his friend with a worried look. "So what now?" he asked nervously, to which Arthur just grinned and put a reassuring arm around his shoulder.

"Leave it to me, Gabe," he replied, then walked toward the throng of young ladies and parents. Arthur raised his arms and spoke to them as though he were a herald: "Welcome, ladies, to your first dance with Good King Gabriel! If you would all please line up along that wall over there," as he said this, he pointed in order to indicate which wall he meant, then continued, "we'll get this test started."

Murmurs erupted from the crowd as they exchanged unsure glances and whispers, but the ladies did as they were told and formed a single file along the left wall. Gabriel stepped forward, looking at his friend, who only winked back at him.

Once the girls were ready, Arthur beckoned the first one in line to come forward. Tentatively she approached them, curtsying low in respect and giving him a small shy smile. She was a petite blonde, perhaps a year younger than Gabriel himself. He recognized her; "Whitney of Saxony-Harcourt, yes?"

"Yes, Your Highness," she giggled.

He bowed to her and took her hand gently, a small smile on his face, before guiding her out into the middle of the dance floor. Turning to face her, he slid his arm gently around Wilhelmina's waist as he took her left hand in his right. She set her free hand against his shoulder, letting out a small giggle as she looked up at him, her bright blue eyes boring up into his own.

When they were ready, Arthur grinned and gave a small nod to the band, who then began to play a sultry tune. Gabriel couldn't help but grin as he led his partner into a slow waltz about the floor, gracefully pulling her along with every smooth move he made. They danced well together, staying in time with each others' movements and not stepping on each others' toes. While they danced, Gabriel began to ask the girl a few questions; what did she like to do for fun, and what kinds of things would she do if she were queen? The girl was shy, and a hint of blush crossed her nose as she replied to his questions in a quiet tone. From what he could tell, she had answered truthfully and honestly, which satisfied him.

When the music eased to a stop, the two bowed and curtsied to each other gracefully, and Gabriel walked the girl to her parents, whose expression had changed from annoyance to happiness as they smiled and bowed in respect. Then the family turned and left the ballroom, returning to the entrance hall to await their answer. After he watched them leave, Gabriel walked back to his friend's side with a heavy sigh. Arthur saw this and looked at him in concern for a second, then grinned mischievously and patted Gabriel on the shoulder.

"You looked like you were having fun out there, Gabe," Arthur said, but Gabriel's smile faded into a look of uncertainty.

"I don't think she's the one," he replied.

"Why not?"

"She doesn't want to be a bride," Gabriel said. "She wants to be a queen, and she doesn't like sitting on the sidelines while someone else is making decisions."

Arthur gave him an understanding nod and turned back to the other girls lined against the wall. "Do you wish to continue, Your Highness?" he asked as importantly as he could, which made the young prince chuckle lightly.

"Of course," Gabriel replied. "It would be rude not to." Arthur nodded and went to fetch the next candidate.

After a few hours, Gabriel finally finished dancing with each of the girls. Some had been excited and giggly, while others were stoic or annoyed, and yet others were shy or hardly spoke at all. The dances never lasted long, but they were long enough to get enough information to help Gabriel determine whether one of the ladies would be a good fit as his queen.

As the last girl left, blowing Gabriel a small kiss, Arthur strode up to his friend and cocked an eyebrow at him. "Tired yet, Gabe?"

"If I never dance again, I'll die happy," Gabriel growled, bending down to rub his aching feet. Arthur laughed at the response, patting his friend's back lightly.

"Well it's over for now." he replied, giving Gabriel a catty grin, "So, which girl did you choose?"

Gabriel stood up straight, frowning. "None of them."

"What?" Arthur responded. "What do you mean, 'none of them'?"

"Just what I said," Gabriel shot back. "None of them is good enough to be my queen. As nice as some of them were, they all wanted power, money, or both. They would get that if I marry any one of them, and I don't want to marry someone who only wants me for what I have. I want to be with someone who likes me for who I am. You know, personality, looks, wisdom, all that mushy adult stuff." He crossed his arms in annoyance, staring absentmindedly through one of the extremely tall windows that looked out over the castle grounds. None of the girls he had danced with seemed to be the right fit, the right girl to share the throne with him.

His mind wandered from those girls to a blonde whose face was dirty, but whose eyes were gentle and kind, her smile sunny and pleasant, always seeming to light up the room when he saw her. She smelled of raspberries and hay, a comforting smell that made him relax whenever he was around her.

Gabriel shook himself from his thoughts and turned to his best friend, who was giving him a look of concern and curiosity, to which the young prince said wryly, "I'll know the girl when I see her, but for now, let's not worry about it so much." This made Arthur furrow his brow even further; but he simply chuckled and smiled to the young king. Then the boys waved to the band, thanking them for their help, and turned to exit the room.

Just as the they were about to take their leave, the sound of heels clicking on the hardwood floor resounded about the dance hall. They both turned to find a red-faced David Whittenburg briskly walking toward them. He looked frustrated, and as he stopped in front of Arthur and Gabriel, he paused for a moment to catch his breath. When he had recovered slightly, he scowled and looked at Gabriel. "There you are, Your Highness!" he exclaimed, still breathing a little hard, "What have you been doing all day? Your next trial is to take place very soon, and it would be unkingly to show up late, or not at all!" He sounded rather cross with the young prince, who looked down at the floor in dismay.

Arthur, seeing his friend feeling terrible, spoke up. "Lord Whittenburg, it's my fault. I dragged him into this—"

"I don't want to hear it, Arthur," Whittenburg snapped, which made both the boys jump in surprise a little. Sighing, Whittenburg turned on his heels and shook his head. "No matter. Please follow me, Your Highness." With that, he strode quickly out of the ballroom before waiting for an answer. The boys looked at each other in surprise. Never had they known Whittenburg to sound so angry at either of them. *I don't think he means to sound mad... But he did sound irritated... I better go after him, before he gets really mad at me,* Gabriel thought to himself, and he gave a small nod to his friend, who returned the gesture. Then he left the ballroom, swiftly following his adviser.

CHAPTER 6

SUMMIT

Only the sound of their footsteps upon the floor could be heard as the two walked through to the entrance hall. Gabriel had his head hung in embarrassment and worry. He had no idea what was in store for him, but he imagined it would involve more decision-making, and a lot of prying eyes judging him with every word that escaped his lips. The mere thought of it made his skin crawl with anxiety. "Don't worry, Sire," Whittenburg said over his shoulder to the young man. "This will be painless and easy. All you really have to do is decide upon diplomatic matters." To Gabriel, this sounded harder than the old man strolling casually ahead of him portrayed it to be.

Whittenburg turned sharply toward the tall tower that housed Gabriel's bedroom. The young man quickly followed him up the cobblestone steps. Where they were going Gabriel had never seen or stepped foot in before, and he was beginning to over think his situation once again, worrying that he would make a mess of things.

The two climbed higher and higher, past windows that looked out upon the courtyard, past smoky torches lighting the spaces between the windows, past the oaken door that marked Gabriel's bedchamber, and on toward the summit. The gray stones looked more weathered than ever as they descended higher into the tower, but perhaps that was Gabriel's imagination playing tricks on him. Soon, he could hear voices echoing ahead, though they weren't very loud, and as they reached the top of the steps, Gabriel peered around in amazement; the gray stone of the walls looked fresher and cleaner in this hall than in the stairwell, and a beautiful dark cherry-wood floor to rival the ballroom's glistened in the sunlight that filtered in through the wide satin-curtained windows. It was the most elegantly decorated of the tower's hallways, for it hosted some of the most important people currently in the kingdom—including Whittenburg, a variety of kings from other nations, and the Captain of the Royal Guard, Sir Kameran Whitetail.

As he looked around in astonishment, Gabriel felt himself being gently pushed from behind toward the end of the grand hallway, which was lined with portraits of royal families from previous years. As he looked, he spotted one that brought back many memories, both good and bad. The portrait included himself as a toddler, held by his mother, the late Queen Alexandra, a beautiful lady whose long, curly brown locks flowed down her back and whose clear blue eyes could make even the worst of liars tell the truth. Beside her stood a tall, burly man, the late King Gregory, Gabriel and Reginald's father. He was known for being kind-hearted and yet stern, and his deeds of war and valor were known far and wide.

As the young king looked upon the portrait, his father's cerulean eyes stared back at him, a strong and yet gentle look in them. Gabriel turned his attention downward, and he saw in the picture a younger version of his older brother, happily smiling as he looked at the infant Gabriel. At this, Gabriel's eyes welled up with tears. At the thought of his brother lost out in the world, dead or not, his chest tightened and sadness arose in his heart. He didn't remember much from when he was that young, but he had recognized his brother's love for him even then. He shook his head as he fought back tears, then turned away from the picture and allowed Whittenburg to usher him down the hallway toward the summit room. They stopped just before a large, open doorway adorned with a dark violet curtain that reached to the floor. Gabriel could only guess that this was the summit room that his adviser had mentioned previously. With a small gulp, he pushed the curtain aside and slipped inside.

The first interesting thing that Gabriel noticed as he entered the room was that it was dark; there were no windows, but in each corner of the room a torch had been lit, illuminating the wooden floor and the oaken table in the middle of the room. It was rather short, with only enough room for a handful of people to seat themselves around it, and the seats themselves were made of oak as well. In those seats were only a few men; most he didn't recognize, but there were a few he thought he remembered. One man Gabriel didn't recognize at all, and gave him a puzzled look. This man had brilliant red hair and beard, almost the color of Arthur's, and dark brown eyes. He was smiling, an expression greatly lacking among the other delegates.

"That is Ericson, Duke of Limerick," Whittenburg replied to Gabriel's unasked question, whereupon Gabriel nodded and turned back to the others who lined the table. Whittenburg then began explaining the other attendees and their whereabouts. There were dukes and rulers and people of power, as well as advisers from other countries. Two of the Council members were also attending the meeting, more than likely to see how well he would do. At this, Gabriel's stomach churned in knots. He was more nervous than ever now. His adviser must have noticed how unnerved he looked, for Gabriel felt the old man's hand come down on his shoulders once again, which caused him to gaze up at Whittenburg, who only smiled.

"Fear not, Your Highness," he said, "I will be here should you need anything. You will do just fine."

Though the old man had faith in him, Gabriel himself wasn't so sure he was up for the job. *However*, he thought to himself, *this will put me one step closer to officially becoming king, so I must do it*. He walked to the edge of the table and stopped, clearing his throat to get everyone's attention. Instantly, all eyes were upon him. As Gabriel glanced around at the guests, he noticed that most of them were giving him looks of distaste, distrust, and uncertainty. He tried to ignore them and began to speak to the room.

"Welcome, everyone," he began in a calm, strong tone. "I would like to thank you all for attending this summit meeting." There were a few murmurs, but they were quickly hushed as he continued, "As you know, King Reginald, my brother, was recently lost in battle, and I am his heir-presumptive. I understand that not everyone thinks allowing me to ascend to the throne is the best course of action, but I wish to prove my worth and become a great king like my brother before me. So, with all due respect, let us start this meeting."

Once again, hushed whispers erupted from some of the delegates, while others simply exchanged an assortment of worried or impatient looks. However, one man rose out of his chair in a haughty fashion and pointed directly at Gabriel. "Men, I ask you, why on God's green Earth are we taking orders from some brat barely out of training pants?"

Gabriel's cheeks flushed in anger, and he was about to shoot an answer back at the rude man when Whittenburg put a hand out in front of him and stepped forward.

"Carlisle, I know this is a bit hard to take in, what with the young king's brother gone and the coronation coming up, but I can assure you, sir, that there is no one better suited for this position than His Majesty, the future King Gabriel."

At this, Carlisle sat back down with his arms crossed in front of his chest, still grumbling in distaste. Gabriel smiled at his adviser from behind; he was thankful he had someone here who believed in him so much. He then cleared his throat as Whittenburg took a step back, nodding in thanks to him, and turned his attention back to the delegates at the table.

"Now then, what is our first order of business?" he asked the room.

This time, everyone fell silent. No one spoke, no one moved; they simply looked around at each other. Then, a chair scuffed and moved as one man raised himself; it was the man with blazing red hair and bright brown eyes, who directed a kind smile toward Gabriel. "Yer Highness," Duke Ericson started, bowing in respect, "I fer one would like t' congratulate ye on yer upcomin' coronation. I think ye'll be a great addition to this council." His thick accent and kind words made Gabriel smile and nod in return.

"Thank you, Duke Ericson."

"I do ha' somethin' that needs t' be taken care of though, lad," Ericson continued as he straightened. "There ha' been many reports of assassination attempts on royals of a' rank of late. Most come from wealthy and well-off families; however, some of the attempts were on townsfolk who associate with these wealthy folks." Once again the room rumbled with more whispers and glances. Gabriel peered around the room at these people; fear and anxiety, along with worry and disbelief, spread across their faces like wildfire. He turned back to Ericson with a serious look upon his face.

"So, how do you plan to catch these blackguards?" he asked calmly.

At that moment, the whole room fell quiet once again. This time, everyone's eyes were on Gabriel and Ericson, who simply grinned at the young man.

"Ah, young Sire, that is where I was a-hopin' t' get yer opinion and counsel," he chuckled, which made Gabriel peer at him curiously, "I need yer help with settin' up a trap t' catch these notorious assassins." Gabriel looked back at his adviser, who simply nodded in acknowledgment, and then he turned back to Ericson with a look of determination.

"What did you have in mind?"

Ericson's grin widened at the remark, and he then proceeded to pull out and unroll a very long piece of parchment, on which was what looked like a blueprint for some kind of odd machine or cage. Diagrams and machinery and other such intricacies were drawn on the parchment, and Gabriel gazed at it curiously as Ericson explained each part. "See here, we lure the assassins in with what they are looking for, then we set up a concealed net and before they know it, they're behin' bars!" He seemed pretty proud of his very simple plan, for he grinned cattily after he had finished. Gabriel pulled away from the blueprint and put a hand on his chin in thought. It was actually simple to set up, and it was straight to the point, but it lacked a sense of secrecy and was by no means foolproof.

"Okay," Gabriel began as he gazed at the paper before him, "but what if they see the net? Or watch you put it up? Assassins are smart; they aren't easily tricked. You would need something a little more elaborate than this..." As he responded, once again the room was abuzz with talk. Whispers of intrigue and interest circulated through the room, and even Ericson showed signs of astonishment. However, he returned to his grinning self and nodded to Gabriel.

"Well then, young man," Ericson started, "How would ye make this better?" Everyone's eyes turned to the young prince, but he didn't even notice; his eyes were set on the blueprint before him, his hand still on his chin in thought.

"Well, first, you would need to figure out just who these people are targeting, and why they're being targeted. Do they have money? Power? Is it for revenge? That way, you can guess who their next target will be and you can be prepared. Once you know who's going to be targeted next, I would station guards at the entrance of every door, and make sure that the windows were secured as well. Assassins are crafty, so you'd want them to think that they'd be getting away scot-free. Then..."

He continued describing what he thought they could do to improve the trap, making sure to consider every angle and opportunity for the assassins to strike, kill, and escape. The idea was to prevent the assassination from happening, but should that fail, they would need a way to prevent them from leaving the scene. As Gabriel rattled off ideas, everyone in the room stared at him, amazed and astonished. Ericson himself was nodding, jotting down notes on another piece of parchment that he had found, scribbling away every word from Gabriel's mouth.

"...And finally, I would hide the nets under each window, preferably next to a tree, and inside the room of the target, in a place where the assassins wouldn't easily notice them." As he finished, he removed his hand from his chin and looked about the room. Everyone remained silent, and those prying eyes he was worried about earlier were anything but prying now; in fact, he could see them staring in amazement. Some of the summit members smiled, while others nodded in approval. Ericson finished his notes and looked at the young man with a big grin.

"Thank ye, Yer Highness," he said in a grateful tone, "Ye don' know how much this'll help wi' the problem."

"I'm just glad to be of help, Lord Ericson," he replied. With another nod, Ericson returned to his seat, looking over what he had scribbled down. No sooner did Ericson sit down before another person stood and looked at Gabriel. To the young man's surprise, it was Sir Kameran, Caitlin's father and captain of the guard. The knight bowed to Gabriel respectfully.

"Your Highness," he began, "It is an honor to be in your presence. I too have a few issues that I would like to discuss with you."

"All right, what seems to be the problem, Sir Kameran?"

Kameran smiled and continued, "First, I would like to bring to your attention the status of the castle walls, Sire. Some of the stones are broken and worn, leaving a sizable hole in the West Wall, and the North Wall needs some minor attention. Secondly, I would like to speak for the troops. They feel as though they need more training, and our weapons and armor are still in poor repair from the war." Gabriel took a moment to take this information in, nodding in response to Sir Kameran's concerns. He turned to look at Whittenburg, who nodded in approval.

"Do you have the resources you need to remedy all this?"

"That's the issue, Sire," Sir Kameran stated. "We lack the supplies with which to make the necessary repairs." At this, Gabriel cast his gaze downward and put his hand to his chin, thinking hard about what Sir Kameran had said. During his studies, he had learned where certain resources could be found and harvested, but the kind of repairs that needed to be made to the walls had to be done as soon as possible, and the stone and mortar required wouldn't be easily available for another three months. As for the troops, he would need to allow them to be trained more, but that meant that he would have to find or promote more trainers, and pay them more money. On top of that, the weapons and armor had to be forged from steel, iron, and silver ores, and if they were lacking in such, the blacksmiths wouldn't be able to do it. It was a tough decision indeed...

Suddenly, he heard a shrill voice among the whispers of curiosity. "

Sire! We could lend you some of our supplies for both of the issues at hand, if you could lend us some manpower." When Gabriel looked to the source of the voice, he saw a short, stout man with a tidy brown beard and matching hair stand up and wave his arm in the air. As Gabriel's brow furrowed curiously, the man continued, "We need more troops to fight off an uprising from a group of bandits." Gabriel once again held his chin and looked down at the ground. This was a bigger decision than he originally had thought. He wasn't just helping someone set up a trap; he would be putting his own men and his own land in danger in order to help another, all because they needed aid and supplies.

It took him a few minutes to respond, but he turned to his guard captain and said with as much authority as he could muster, "Sir Kameran." The knight quickly stood at attention.

"Yes, Sire!"

"Would you be willing to take some troops to... um..." Gabriel looked back over at the man who had spoken up, "Where are you from again, good sir?"

"Eddington, Sire. I am Duke Archibald," said the man, to which Gabriel nodded thankfully, then turned back to Sir Kameran.

"Would you be willing to send your people to Eddington to help out?"

To this, the knight smiled and nodded. "Indeed I would, Sire. For the good of our land, and theirs."

"Thank you, Sir Kameran," Gabriel replied seriously. "Duke Archibald, we accept your proposal."

Archibald gladly smiled and nearly jumped out of his seat as he rushed to Gabriel's side, taking the king's hand in his and shaking it vigorously. "Oh thank you, thank you, Your Highness! We will have those materials sent to you as soon as our affairs are dealt with." This made both Gabriel and Kameran smile, but Gabriel then turned back to his guard captain.

"Now, Sir Kameran, about the training..."

Kameran quickly turned his attention back to the young king, standing tall. "Yes, Sire?"

"Take the soldiers who need the most training with you. This will be an excellent opportunity for them get the real-world experience they require," Gabriel said, "though I doubt a bunch of scurvy bandits will be much of a challenge for your men, sir."

Kameran nodded, smiling broadly. "Thank you, Sire, I will do just that." He sat back down just as Ericson had, and the young man turned to the rest of the summit council, looking around to see if there were any other concerns that needed to be addressed. However, no one else seemed to have anything else to say, so Whittenburg stepped forward and said, "If there are no more concerns...? Very well, then, this concludes this month's summit meeting. Thank you all for attending, and we shall see you in another month."

The delegates filed out of the room one by one, congratulating Gabriel as they did, and thanking him for a wonderful summit meeting—even Carlisle of Glenholly. Gabriel himself was aglow with pride. He had made it through another trial, and had done a fantastic job of it, as far as he could tell. Soon, the summit chamber was empty, except for him and Whittenburg; nothing but the sound of talking in the hallway and their own breathing echoed around the room. It was then that his chief adviser turned to him with a grin. "Well *done*, Your Majesty. I must say that I am impressed," he said.

Gabriel nodded, returning the grin with one of his own. "That was easier than I thought," he replied. The scholar chuckled to himself, then the two turned and left the room behind, passing through the velvet curtain once again.

Outside the room, the excitement had died down a little, and only a few people still milled around the halls. Whittenburg turned to Gabriel, informing him that his duties for today were finished and that in a few days' time, another trial would take place. Though Gabriel groaned, he nodded to the old man. Having said his piece, Whittenburg left Gabriel in the hallway to do as he pleased for the rest of the day. The young man watched as his adviser made his way to his own quarters. *Another trial over,* he thought. *What will come next...?*

As he thought this, he walked toward the staircase that housed his bedchambers, but not before stopping at a particular portrait. He stared up at it, at his older brother, who was much younger in the picture. Many thoughts and concerns raced through Gabriel's mind; had his brother ever felt the same way? Had Reginald felt as though he wasn't going to make it after their parents perished? Would he, Gabriel, be a good king? These and many more questions presented themselves to young Gabriel, but as he remembered the day's events, he couldn't help but think that maybe he could be. He smiled to his brother's painting. "I will make you proud, Reggie, " he said aloud. After all, being in his brother's shadow for all those years had to have paid off a little.

With this thought in his mind, he turned away from the portrait and hurried toward the stairs to find his friends.

CHAPTER 7

SUMMER RAIN

The test of strength that Whittenburg had spoken of was scheduled to take place two days later. Though the prognosticators had predicted a sunny day, it turned out to be a rather dismal, rainy one instead. Gabriel sat in his bed, listening to the sound of the raindrops smashing against his window shutters. He couldn't go to the town square, where he could have spent his day chasing the court felines or checking in with the villagers and shopkeepers. He really couldn't go much of anywhere without fear of catching a cold or getting completely soaked. So there he sat, silently staring out through the half-open window, his hand resting upon his chin, until he heard a soft knock. Jolted out of his mood, he looked to the door; then, surprised and curious, Gabriel got up off his bed and walked over to the door, swinging it open slightly. When he saw the smiling face of Whittenburg, he sighed in annoyance and opened the door further.

"Good morning, Your Highness," said the old man cheerfully, to which the young prince merely snorted and turned his attention back to the window, allowing Whittenburg to enter fully.

"I don't understand what's so good about it, " Gabriel retorted under his breath.

"Well, it seems that the first part of your physical testing is going to have to be moved to a less dismal day, since it requires a dry arena."

Gabriel turned to Whittenburg as he heard this, a smile spreading across his face. "You mean... No trials? No tests? I can do what I want today?"

"Yes indeed, Sire. However, there are still a few things you need to be aware of," he began, but Gabriel wasn't listening. He hurried to his closet and pulled out the most comfortable clothing he could find and slipped into it, all while his adviser was trying to speak with him about something important. He then raced past Whittenburg and down the stairs, waving to him as he went.

"I'll listen to that later, David!"

The old scholar tried to follow him down the stairs, but he wasn't fast enough. "Sire, please, wait! There are some things I simply must discuss with you..." he called after the youth, but his voice trailed off as Gabriel got farther away from him.

Servants and other castle staff were bustling about, performing their normal morning duties, tidying up as well as making sure everything was prepared for Gabriel's upcoming coronation. Just because it was raining didn't mean work stopped in the castle. Most of the preparations had been completed; the banners and decorations lay dormant in the homes of their creators, and the gardeners had finished perfecting their coronation day bouquets. The cake was being planned not only by the head baker of the castle, but by the town's master baker as well, ensuring that it would be a cake fit for a new king.

As Gabriel passed by the throne room, he noticed that a pedestal had been placed next to the king's throne. On it sat the golden crown, gleaming in the morning sun, and the royal ceremonial scepter, used only during the ceremony to swear in the new king. He stopped for a moment to gaze upon these items. He was both excited and nervous about becoming king, but he also felt a deep sense of sadness. Once he donned the crown, everyone would admire him and take him seriously, but at the same time... well, the king was supposed to be Reginald, not him. He felt as if he were taking the crown from his older sibling, even though Reginald—already hailed as Reginald the Lionhearted in the Histories of Halcyon Ridge, despite his relatively brief reign—was thought to be dead.

He sighed as he turned away from the royal items.

The rumbling in his stomach told him it was time to go, and he continued to walk down the hallway toward the kitchens for a much-needed breakfast. As he approached, he savored the scent of fresh bread baking in the stone ovens. Decadent meat dishes of all varieties were simmering over open flames, with hen's eggs, scrambled or otherwise, cooking in cast-iron pans. The aroma made his mouth water profusely, and he licked his lips as he turned a corner and found himself in the kitchen. Smiling, and with stomach growling loudly, the young prince strode further in to find a bite to eat.

"Ho there, young king!" came the cheery voice of a familiar face. Gabriel turned to his left, and his smile widened as he saw Mrs. Fletcher, the stout ginger-haired head cook, making her way toward him.

"Morning!" he called to her.

Hearing the tone of his voice, Mrs. Fletcher laughed heartily. "Hungry are ya, lad?" she said in a chirpy tone, to which Gabriel nodded as his stomach roared once again. The short, round Scottish lady chortled, then turned back into the busy kitchen, to the heart of the pantry, gathering Gabriel a plate of the finest breakfast food he had ever eaten: scrambled eggs seasoned with salt and pepper, cubed fried potatoes, two sizzling slices of bacon, and two slices of freshly baked bread, toasted to perfection and topped with freshly churned butter. It was a meal fit for a king, exactly what he deserved. Just seeing the scrumptious food made him practically drool.

Mrs. Fletcher grinned to Gabriel as she brought the plate over to a small wooden table on the edge of the pantry, where most of the servants took their meal breaks. No one was there at the moment, but even if there had been, Gabriel wouldn't have minded. He enjoyed the company of the lower classes. Maybe it was because they were more down- to-Earth and kinder than most of the people he dealt with, especially to someone who listened to their needs and wants.

He seated himself at the little table, allowing the wonderful aroma to waft into his nostrils. A fork had been placed next to his plate, the only utensil he had ever used when dining with the castle kitchen staff, and he smiled. The meat was tender enough that he never needed a knife. He devoured the succulent meal quickly, a contented sigh escaping his lips when he was finished. "Thanks again, Mrs. Fletcher," Gabriel said as the stout cook walked over to him.

She laughed once again and bowed slightly. "Any time, Your Highness," she replied respectfully, then scooted away to finish the meals for the rest of the castle. Gabriel cleaned up his own mess, having done it quite often when his brother was around; then, with his own satisfied smile, he bounded out of the kitchens and toward the entrance hall.

The palace wasn't as quiet as it had been earlier. As he strode through the hall, admiring the hard work of his soon-to-be subjects and servants, he noticed that he was alone; Caitlin and Arthur hadn't come to see him, nor had they come to breakfast yet, he noted as he glanced into the dining hall. They often seemed to be missing at the same time lately. Curious as to their whereabouts, he left the dining hall and began to search for his comrades in the places he knew they frequented the most.

His search began in the ballroom, just down the hall from the throne room and dining hall. As he looked about for his companions, he could hear no one but the band beginning to practice for the day. Normally, on a rainy day like this, the three friends would come in and make all kinds of trouble for the royal band, playing their instruments without permission and mixing up their sheet music. Otherwise, they might play hide and seek; Caitlin always won because she could be the quietest, whereas Arthur and Gabriel's laughter echoed about the high ceiling. Gabriel entered the room, his footsteps resounding off of the walls, and began to look for his friends. He searched behind the chairs, instruments, music stands, curtains, and everywhere he could think of. He even asked the band if they had seen Arthur and Caitlin, but they shook their heads. Sighing to himself, puzzlement still upon his face, Gabriel left the ballroom to search elsewhere.

As he walked back through the entrance hall, he stopped and peered back into the dining hall. Maybe he had missed them the first time, but as he walked to the door to look around, several nobles were walking out, blocking his view. He did notice that Sir Kameran was still eating; he and Whittenburg were discussing something amusing from the way they were acting, laughing and smiling as they were. Gabriel took one more look around, seeing that they weren't there, and left the dining room to go onto the next place. However, as he turned back toward the stone staircase, he realized that he could have simply asked Sir Kameran about his daughter's whereabouts. At this thought, he shrugged his shoulders and kept on walking.

His trek up the granite stairs brought him to his bedchamber. Perhaps they were waiting for him in here, ready to throw his door open and surprise him. However, as he opened the large wooden door, looking around his bedroom, he saw no one. The messy sheets he had left this morning had already been replaced, and his soiled clothing had been taken for washing. The shutters had been closed, so no rain would get into the room and soak or ruin everything. The maids had been here, but no Caitlin and no Arthur. Sighing once again, he closed the door to his bedchamber, locking it and walking deeper into the castle.

He climbed the stairs further to the summit room, then ventured down to the lowest sections of the castle, even into the dank, dirty, empty dungeons; but his friends weren't anywhere he looked. He checked his room again; no luck. His confusion turned into frustration and annoyance, and as he descended the granite staircase again, he sat himself down on the last step, his hand on his chin in puzzlement. Where could they be? They were nowhere in the castle...

As he thought this, Gabriel's eyes rested upon the portcullis. Anything else he could try was outside, maybe in the courtyard or in the stables, or even in town. He wondered over to the large door, which was closed so the rain wouldn't come inside. Jackets, coats, and rain boots sat near the entrance for anyone who wished to exit into the drizzling mist. Gabriel quickly and quietly slipped one of the rain jackets over his shoulders, flipped the hood over his mahogany head, and pushed his way out.

Gabriel closed the door with some difficulty, then turned and looked upon the drizzly dismal day. Everything was soaked in a light coating of rain, the sun gone from the sky, or so it seemed, as gray clouds scudded across the brighter patch of gray where it should have been. Little puddles had formed in the crevices of the cobblestone path as well. Gabriel smiled and walked along the pathway until he reached a part that branched off into the gardens. The hedges dripped with water, and the flowers drooped low, heavy with the rain. Here, Gabriel looked about to see if he could find his friends, but still they were nowhere to be seen. Sighing to himself in disappointment, he began to walk back toward the entrance of the keep, and took a quick stroll down to the town square below.

When he arrived there, Gabriel was surprised to see that some of the shopkeepers' stalls were still open, even though it was such a damp day. He was even more surprised to see that a few were fairly busy; the florist and the baker were both selling their wares indoors, and the blacksmith still had his weapons on display, though in the windows of his shop instead of out on the display stands. There were a lot of customers inside the bakery, probably getting buns or some other kind of breakfast foods, and they all looked rather unhappy or annoyed. Quickly, Gabriel peered in through the side window, dripping wet as it was, searching among the throng of people; but he still couldn't spot his comrades. He frowned both in confusion and annoyance, and turned away from the window, leaning against the side of the building. Where could they be? The only place he hadn't checked yet was... His frown dissipated into a wide grin, and the young king raced off toward the castle once again.

By now it was mid-afternoon, and the stone walkway he had descended to the square earlier was more wet and puddle-ridden than when he had first started, and he had to tread even more carefully as he ran. The prince even slipped a couple of times, catching himself before he fell. As he neared the castle gates, he turned down a different path before the courtyards, and found himself headed down toward the stables and armory. He hoped to find Arthur and Caitlin within the warm, inviting walls of the barn. The scent of hay and manure filled the air as Gabriel entered the high-ceilinged structure, sighing happily. Some of the horses whinnied and shied away from their handlers once or twice, though most were lying down or munching away happily on oats and hay. As the staff noticed his presence, they bowed low. He returned the gesture and kept walking down the row of stalls, looking into each to see if he could spy his friends.

"Your Majesty?" came a gentle voice in front of him, one he knew well. Gabriel looked up from his search and smiled even more broadly as a blonde maiden came into his view.

"Hello, Ashlyn," he responded, and saw a blush crawling across her nose as he spoke to her. She turned her face downward and smiled bashfully at him.

"H-hello, Your Highness," she stuttered, twisting her foot into the hay on the floor as she returned her gaze to his face, "What brings you down here on such a dreary day?"

Gabriel grinned. "You can call me Gabriel, Ashlyn, if it's easier," he reminded her, at which she blushed even more, then continued, "I came to find my friends, Arthur and Caitlin. Have you seen them?"

"No, Si-... I mean, Gabriel," she quickly corrected herself, shaking her head. "I haven't seen either of them today. It's been pretty quiet down here so far." At this, Gabriel raised a hand to his chin in thought. It was possible that Arthur and Caitlin were at their own houses; he hadn't thought to check there. Shrugging, he smiled to the girl.

"Well, since I have nothing to do today, why don't you and I do something?" he asked, which brought the pink right back to her already rosy cheeks.

"W-well, I-I don't know..." Ashlyn uttered in a nervous tone, looking behind her as though looking for permission. A taller, darker-haired lady looked their way, and she smiled and nodded to Ashlyn, almost as if giving her a silent okay. To this, Ashlyn smiled gratefully to the woman and turned back to the young man before her, stating, "Well, I guess it wouldn't hurt to take a day off every once in a while."

A grin spread across Gabriel's face, and he took her small hand in his. "Great! Follow me, then!" he cried in excitement, which startled the horses a little, and the two took off toward the entrance of the barn. Ashlyn grabbed a rain coat and an umbrella, then the two rushed out into the drizzly, rainy afternoon.

The young king pulled his new friend up to the castle entrance, but before they got to the oaken door that led inside the tall stony structure, Gabriel made a sharp right, and took Ashlyn down into the castle courtyards, where the gardens were. Ashlyn had clearly never been to this part of the castle before; her eyes seemed to light up as she looked around. Even though it was raining, the gardenias and amaryllis were still impressive in their multitude of colors, littering the hedges and stony pathway, and morning glories and ivy clung to the gray walls of the castle, climbing almost as high as Gabriel's bedchamber window. Tulips and marigolds lined the path as well, and as they walked further on, they found themselves in the center of the gardens.

"This is so beautiful," Ashlyn commented, her jaw dropped in amazement, lips upturned in a shy smile. This made Gabriel smile slightly, turning to look at the flowers dripping with water.

"It's even more beautiful when it's sunny," he responded.

They kept walking until they reached a small fountain in the middle of the garden. Completely made of marble, it only stood a few feet taller than Gabriel, with a wide base the two could easily sit on, and a small, fanned-out top, almost like a bird bath. Ashlyn stopped to admire it, tracing her fingers delicately along the intricate designs on the base of the fountain, a smile pasted on her pale face. Gabriel noticed how happy she looked, and grinned. He liked seeing her happy and smiling—not scared or nervous, but confident and beautiful in her own special way. Just then, Gabriel put a hand to his chest, looking down at it curiously. His whole torso felt warm, as though a fire had been kindled in his ribcage. Could he really be...

He shook his head and looked at the blonde girl, who was still grinning. Ashlyn turned back to look at him, only to see him gazing at her in admiration, and it caused her cheeks to burn bright pink. "W-Why are you looking at me like that?" she asked tentatively. This made Gabriel snap out of his gaze; he blinked a few times and looked away, scratching his head sheepishly.

"Oh, uh, n-no reason..." the young king stuttered. He never fumbled for words, especially with girls. His reaction made Ashlyn laugh out loud heartily, her short hair tossing as she did. Her laugh made Gabriel smile and forget about his embarrassment.

"Oh, Gabriel," she said through a chuckle, "You certainly are different from your devious cousin." Just as the words spilled from her lips, her eyes widened and her smile faded, and she raised her hands to her mouth, covering it in shame. Gabriel could see the hurt and worry in her eyes, so he slid over to her and took her hands in his.

"Ash, it's all right," he said with a gentle smile. "I hate him, too." The girl smiled slightly at this, but then turned her gaze to the ground, as though ashamed of what she had said. Gabriel squeezed her hands gently and continued, "What was it like? Serving under him... If you don't mind me asking."

At this, she let out a long, drawn-out sigh, her eyes still averted from his.   "It was awful..." she responded sadly, looking up at the sky while droplets of rain fell upon her pale face. "He was cruel and unforgiving... and..." Her voice trailed off as she stared off into space. Gabriel tilted his head to the side curiously.

"And what?" he pried, as Ashlyn turned away from him completely, putting her wet hands on her forearms, hugging herself tightly.

"He wanted things that I wouldn't give him," she said in a rush. "And he did demeaning things to me... Far worse than anything I could have ever imagined." Gabriel could see her physically shudder at the mere mention of it, and his heart wrenched at the thought. His cousin, abusive to women? Though he wouldn't have put abuse past Ayden, Gabriel had hoped he was better behaved than that. Anger and sadness swirled in him, before Ashlyn spoke once more. "I'm still scared he may do something to me for leaving... He..."

Before she could say more, Gabriel reached out, took her firmly by the arm, and turned her to face him. They were now staring at each other, eye-to-eye, Ashlyn with a look of surprise and Gabriel with a mixture of emotions, mostly determination. "Ashlyn, I swear on my family name that I will NEVER let him hurt you again—or anyone else in my kingdom, for that matter."

"B-but, Gab-" Before she could respond farther, Gabriel leaned in close and closed his eyes.

The rain splashed down around them, but he couldn't have known that, or felt the drops upon his bare mahogany head; for he was enraptured as his lips pressed gently against Ashlyn's in a deep, meaningful kiss. The warmth of her lips against his filled him with a burning mixture of emotions, and his hands moved from her arms to around her waist, holding her close in a warm, inviting embrace. Ashlyn's eyelids slowly fell, her own arms slipping around Gabriel's neck. Rain fell soft and light around them, making the scene all the more magical.

As their lips parted and their eyes opened, they realized what had happened and quickly pulled away from each other, deep blushes spreading like wildfire across their faces. *What was I thinking?!* Gabriel thought to himself, reaching up to touch his lips. The kiss had left him filled with a wonderful feeling, almost like it had happened all on its own. He lowered his hand and looked over to the beautiful girl beside him, whose hair was drenched with rain and whose head was hanging slightly. However, as he peered closer, he could see the hint of a smile upon her face, her hand also pressed to her lips fondly. Had she enjoyed it as much as he had? The only way to find out was to ask, but he was nervous; What would she say? The fact that she hadn't run away was a good sign.

Tentatively he began to speak. "Ashlyn... I..."

"It's all right, Gabriel," she said quickly but softly, turning to him with a sincere smile, her bright sapphire eyes glowing. "You don't have to apologize."

Gabriel sighed in relief and gave her a grin of his own. "Thank you," he replied, saying no more.

The two of them turned away from each other for a few moments, and Gabriel finally got the nerve up to speak again, clearing his throat and grasping her hand, entwining her fingers with his own. "Let's get you home, then, hmm?" To this, Ashlyn nodded, though reluctantly, and the two of them walked back through the beautifully wet gardens toward the stables.

As they entered the warm, dry barn, Ashlyn shed her wet jacket, and they proceeded to walk down toward the staff quarters. They kept silent the entire way, but the smiles on their faces were undeniable. The other stable hands who passed were curious, giving the two puzzled looks, but they said nothing and continued to walk on. Once they had reached her bedchamber, they released hands, and Ashlyn turned to him.

"Thank you, Gabriel, for today..." Her hands twisted the hem of her tunic nervously, the blush returning to her nose once again.

Gabriel chuckled a little and bowed to her, as a gentleman would after a day out with a beautiful lady. "No, Ashlyn, thank you," he responded, causing her to giggle like a young girl. "Today was fantastic. Thank you for spending it with me."

"Any time, Your Highness," Ashlyn replied with a curtsy, then turned to her door, opening it slowly. Before disappearing behind it, she looked at him. "I hope we can do it again sometime soon." With that, the door closed behind her, and she was gone.

Gabriel shook his head fondly and turned, walking back through the barn toward the castle. "As do I, Ash."

Later that night, Gabriel finally met up with his companions. "Where have you been all day?!" cried Caitlin.

"Yeah, we were worried something had happened to you!" Arthur agreed in a loud voice.

"I could say the same about you," he retorted. "I couldn't find you anywhere this morning." As they exchanged nervous glances, Gabriel sighed and shook his head as he sat beside his two friends in the dining hall, just staring at the food before him. He couldn't get Ashlyn out of his mind. "Anyway, I was visiting someone," he said finally, scooping a small helping of mashed potatoes on his spoon.

Caitlin and Arthur gave each other a puzzled look, then cast a wary one to their friend. "Visiting...?" Arthur asked.

"With who?" Caitlin insisted.

"With a very special person," Gabriel replied, then brought the spoon to his mouth savoring the creamy potatoes.

The two pals were again confused. "Who was it?" Caitlin demanded, making Gabriel sigh again.

He looked around the room at the others eating with him, then turned to his friends and whispered. "That girl we helped. Ashlyn."

"WHAT?!?!" they cried.

Everyone in the room turned their way, and Gabriel smiled sheepishly to them, then scowled at his friends. "Hush, would you!" he snapped.

"Sorry," responded Arthur.

"Well, come on," Caitlin said insistently, "Don't leave out any details. Tell us what happened!"

Gabriel explained how he'd looked for the two of them, and unable to find his companions, he decided to go to the stables, where he found Ashlyn and went on a small... date, with her. Arthur and Caitlin's eyes lit up. "What happened then?" Caitlin asked anxiously.

"Well..." Gabriel began, thinking back on that moment that he and Ashlyn had shared in the garden, smiling fondly at the memory. Arthur and Caitlin could see the look of affection in their comrade's eyes and smirked.

"Ha, I know where this is going," Arthur said playfully.

Gabriel heard him and blushed profusely, scowling once again. "Shut it, Red!"

"Well, *I* think it's adorable," Caitlin responded, a gleam in her hazel eyes, "Our fair kinglet is in love with a lowly peasant girl."

Arthur snorted with laughter. "Kinglet?"

At this, Gabriel put a finger to his lips. "Shh, both of you! I don't want the whole world to know!"

"Don't worry, Gabe," Arthur chuckled, "We won't tell a soul."

"Promise?"

"Promise," both his friends replied, raising their pinkies in a salute. At this, Gabriel smiled. He knew he could count on his friends for everything, even keeping a secret.

Later, after dinner, Gabriel dragged his tired self up to his bedchamber. The room felt a bit stuffy, so he went to the window and threw it open. Then he slipped out of his still-damp clothing, and pulled on a fresh pair of undergarments and pajamas. Sighing heavily, he then flung himself onto his bed and under his covers. A new day would start tomorrow, and he would have to go back to his training and trials; but for this night, he would let himself be at ease. Memories of the day's events passed through his head as he reminisced, and soon he'd drifted happily into a dream-filled slumber.

CHAPTER 8

IT'S JOUST A GAME!
(PART 1)

"Rise and shine, sleepyhead!"

"Ugh..." Gabriel groaned as he heard the loud announcement in his ear. *Morning already?* he thought as he pulled the covers down just past his chin. Rubbing his eyes tiredly, he glanced up to see who had so rudely awoken him. There stood bubbly blonde Caitlin, grinning broadly.

"Caitlin, why are you up so early?" the king asked in a snippy tone. Caitlin didn't seem to mind, or perhaps she hadn't noticed his tone of voice, and she walked cheerily toward his wardrobe to find him some clothing, throwing open the doors and fiddling with some of the shirts.

"Whittenburg sent me to get you," she responded, "Your first physical trial is waiting outside in the training arena. You need to look the part." She rummaged through the pants and other articles of clothing, shaking her head as she found things that wouldn't seem suitable.

Keeping his lower half covered, Gabriel grumbled, "What does that old rogue have planned for me this time?" He then realized they were missing a certain someone as he looked around his bedroom. "Hey, where's Arthur? What would people think if they knew you were in my room alone with me? They might talk."

Caitlin snorted as she pulled out a dark maroon button-up shirt and tossed it to the bed, which the young monarch lazily reached for and slid over his head. "Should've thought about that before sweeping Ashlyn away, *alone*, for your little tryst yesterday."

"Why? Are you jealous?"

She whirled, red-faced, and put her fists on her hips. "I am NOT jealous! I'm already s—" she caught herself with an obvious effort, and continued, "Arthur is waiting outside. He's going to take you to where your trial will take place." She tossed a pair of pants at him, hitting him in the face. "I'm going to go help set everything up after this."

Gabriel picked up the pants she had lobbed, but didn't bother to put them on yet. He only gave her a confused look, wondering what his adviser had in store for him, and then gave Caitlin an even more puzzled look as she brought over a pair of elegant black riding boots and long stockings.

"What are those for?"

"You'll see," was Caitlin's answer as she walked toward the door, resting her hand upon the handle, "Come on, now, there's no time to waste. Arthur will be waiting out here for you. See you soon!" Having said this, she slipped out through the door and closed it behind her.

Gabriel slid the covers off his lower body and finished dressing himself. He donned the light-brown breeches that had been thrown to him, and then slid the long, thin hose over his feet and up his legs. He hated wearing hose; it made him feel like a fop. Finally, he slipped the riding boots on and stood up on the velvet rug, wiggling his toes to see if everything fit right. Smiling at his handiwork, he walked to the window and pushed the half-open shutters against the outer walls. The sun was shining brightly, warming everything in its wake. Sighing, Gabriel let the gentle rays soak into his skin, taking in the freshness of the day. "All right," he stated to no one in particular, then turned from the window and walked out of his room.

Arthur stood against the far wall just outside the door, his arms crossed and one leg propped up against the stone behind him. His eyes were closed and he looked as if he was deep in thought. As the door to Gabriel's bedchamber creaked open, he lifted his ginger head and grinned. The two exchanged a nod of understanding, and Arthur pulled himself away from the wall, beginning the short descent to the entrance hall, with a curious Gabriel hot on his heels. Gabriel was feeling slightly more confident than usual, but he was still worried about what his next trial would be. All he could tell so far was that the trial would take place outside, and that it involved riding a horse, as Caitlin had dug out his riding boots. *But what could it be?* he wondered. A race, perhaps? But what would be the significance of a horse race? That didn't prove anything except how fast your horse was, and how well you could maintain your balance.

More questions gathered in his mind as they reached the bottom of the stairs and took a right toward the ballrooms and the kitchens. Everyone was busy completing the usual morning duties, as well as preparing delicious meals to be had after the test, whatever it was. Gabriel had to admire their diligence and hard work. As the castle staff saw their "kinglet" striding by, they smiled and nodded or bowed in respect, then quickly returned to their duties.

Smiling and waving, the two friends continued down the hallway toward the rear entrance of the castle, passing the kitchens and servant's quarters before exiting through a small oak door. The light of the sun filtered through the crack of the door as Gabriel swung it open slowly, illuminating the gray stone. He could hear the sound of fanfare and cheering coming from outside; and then, the arena where the test would take place came into view. It was a tall structure made of the same stone as the castle, all surrounding a Colosseum-style arena field. It was usually used for the annual Grand Tournament, but not much more.

While Gabriel had been staring at the arena absentmindedly, Arthur had walked past him briskly, calling back to Gabriel when he realized his friend had stopped. Gabriel snapped out of his trance and hurried after his friend. "So, figured it out yet, Gabe?" he asked, to which Gabriel only shook his head in annoyance.

"No, but I have a feeling it involves horses," he replied.

Arthur nodded and turned back to the path ahead of him, humming softly to himself as he did. Gabriel rolled his eyes and quickened his pace to keep up with him.

They soon reached the tall stone archway that led into the arena's entrance. Gabriel examined the intricate designs and patterns carved into the stone here, so unlike at the castle. The only times he had passed through this arch had been to watch his brother compete in jousting matches and horse races. Memories of Reginald floated back to his mind—memories of watching his brother barrel down the arena racetrack at top speed on his white mare, or stabbing his opponents with the hard end of the lance, grinning at the competition as he leaned into each turn or celebrated each victory. Gabriel could still hear the cheers and applause in the stands from the crowd of bystanders and spectators as Reginald crossed the finish line at stunning speeds, and as he remembered this, he could feel the same old feelings arise in his chest: Admiration, love, fondness, pride... A smile spread across his face, and his heart and mind were aglow as he remembered those moments as if they had happened yesterday.

"Hey! Gabe!" came Arthur's voice. Gabriel shook himself to full attention and looked at his friend, who was already five steps ahead of him. As he neared his companion, Arthur gave him a puzzled look. "What's going on? Are you okay?"

"Yeah, I'm all right," Gabriel responded, taking one long look back at the stone archway, "Just... remembering, that's all."

Arthur nodded. "Yeah, I understand. Come on, it's this way. Lord Whittenburg won't like it if we're late." As they hurried on, Arthur continued, "You'll need Solstice for this, and Ashlyn has taken great care of him for you." At the mention of the blonde's name, Gabriel smiled a little. Arthur saw this and winked, then led his regal pal down the right-hand path toward the arena stables, where the loud sound of stamping hooves and whinnying horses could be heard..

Gabriel was surprised to note that in the stables, tapestries very like those that hung in the castle now lined the dreary gray stones. The floor here, however, was coated with a thin layer of sawdust and dirt, to make the path easier on the horses' hooves. The two boys entered through another tall gray archway, and their nostrils were flooded with the aromas of hay, oats, manure, and oiled leather. Gabriel marched toward the special stall that housed his black-and-white paint stallion. It had been a gift to him from his parents, and Gabriel loved the horse nearly as much as he loved his brother.

It didn't take long before he could hear the loud whinny of a horse being a bit unruly. He picked up his pace a little, and when he was within a few paces of the animal, he raised two fingers to his mouth and gave a loud whistle. The horse stopped in its tracks and looked in his direction, instantly calming itself enough to allow the handlers to put a lead rope on its halter. Once Gabriel had reached his horse, the stable lads handed the lead rope off to him, bowed respectfully, and left him with the big animal. The two of them looked at each other for a while, then the horse gave him a gentle nudge on the shoulder, as if he were trying to say hello and convey his feelings of loneliness.

"I know you've missed me, Solstice," Gabriel started, patting the horse's muzzle gently, bringing forth a loud snort from the stallion. "I've been so busy with this king business, I haven't been paying attention to you, have I?" The horse merely nudged his arm again with his answer. Gabriel chuckled, laying his head against the horse, who didn't seem to mind and just snorted once again, yanking his head downward to nibble at the hay on the ground. Gabriel smiled. He had a feeling that Solstice knew more about him than anyone else in the kingdom did.

"Come on, ol' boy," he ushered to the horse, who lifted his head sharply and turned; then the two of them walked down to the end of the stables together. On a bench there sat a shining suit of armor, golden-bright and glistening with polish. A saddle and bridle had been set aside for Solstice, which Gabriel took and easily slipped onto the horse. Solstice moved only slightly, seemingly unaffected by Gabriel's light tugging and pulling here and there. For a king, Gabriel was rather used to doing things on his own, including saddling up his own horse. He remembered the times he used to sneak out of the castle at night to go on night-time rides, only to be caught by his brother. However, instead of scolding him, Reggie would saddle up and go riding with him. It was another reason why Gabriel loved, and missed, his brother dearly. Trying to push the memory into the back of his mind, he finished tightening Solstice's harnesses and bit, and, satisfied with his work, turned to the oaken bench.

The shining yellow metal sat in the late morning light of day, gleaming mellowly. Its wasn't solid gold—gold was too heavy and soft to work as armor—but it was thickly gilded. Seeing its golden exterior, Gabriel couldn't help but think about his last moments with his brother, Reggie's own gleaming golden armor shining in the early morning sun. As he remembered those final moments, he wiped a tear from his eye and looked down at the armor with a new-found determination. Reggie wouldn't want to see him crying and feeling sorry for himself. He would have wanted Gabriel to get up in the saddle, ride into the stadium, and take the realm by storm. Nodding to himself, he slipped into the metal suit, one piece at a time.

The armor was heavy and uncomfortable, and he had to call in a stable lad to help him tighten all the buckles and hold things in place. *How can the knights wear this stuff all day long?* Gabriel wondered as he pulled the breastplate over his torso, fastening it to his sides. Next, he and his helper tightened on the leg guards, the greaves, making sure they wouldn't slip off as he was riding. On his arms went the vambraces and cowters that protected his elbows and forearms. Finally, he slid on the heavy metal gauntlets, wiggling his fingers to make sure they fit right. The insides of the gauntlets were lined with soft doeskin, to keep his fingers warm and for maximum mobility. Sighing to himself, he dismissed the lad, then reached for the gleaming golden helmet left on the bench. He stared at it for a few moments, unsure whether to put it on then or wait until after he had mounted the horse. He decided to do the latter. He unfastened Solstice's bridle from where it was hitched, and began to lead his steed out toward the arena.

"Gabriel!" cried a voice from behind him just as he was about to leave for the arena entrance. Gabriel stopped, turning as he heard the patter of small feet racing up from his rear. The yellow hair was the first thing he saw, and he smiled as Ashlyn came to a halt before him, panting slightly. Her sapphire eyes stared at him and Solstice in awe. "Wow, you two look amazing." Upon seeing her, Solstice gave a small snort and nudged her fondly, which made Ashlyn giggle a little.

"Thanks, Ashlyn, and thank you for taking care of Solstice for me," he replied, which caused the stable "lad" to blush brightly.

"It was nothing, really..." she said shyly, twisting her foot into the ground timidly, "Um... g-good luck out there today..."

"Yeah. I'm gonna need it," Gabriel responded. Ashlyn only nodded with a timid smile, and turned back around, racing down the way she had come. Gabriel shook his head fondly, then turned and walked toward the arena entrance.

The fanfare grew louder as he approached the stone arch, cheers and shouts echoing through the small opening. Gabriel felt a tightness in his chest, and he began to feel a little nervous about what would await him in this trial. He noticed a familiar figure standing near the door, and sighed in relief as he realized who it was.

"Greetings, Sire," Sir Kameran said to him with a smile and a low bow, to which Gabriel only nodded in return. "I see you are ready for your jousting match today."

Gabriel's eyes widened slightly. "Jousting match? Why don't people tell me these things?" He looked up at his horse, whose expression remained undaunted, then back to Sir Kameran. "No one told me this was going to be a jousting match."

The knight merely smiled and patted Gabriel on the back. "Ah, but that is part of being a king, Sire," he retorted, "You have to be prepared for anything thrown your way."

Gabriel's gaze dropped; he knew that the man was right. He looked back at Sir Kameran with that same look of determination as before and nodded. "Very well, then," he said sternly, "What do I have to do?"

"All you have to do," Sir Kameran said with a small smile and a nod,

"Is knock your opponent off his horse with your lance. You've practiced that for years. Do it to three opponents, and you win; but should you fall even once, then you fail the test."

"I haven't trained specifically for this," Gabriel said. He could feel a heavy lump form in his stomach. He knew how to joust, but it wasn't one of his strengths, and the thought of failure frightened him.

"That, too, is part of the test," Kameran noted. "But you know the basics, aye?"

Gabriel glared at the knight captain. "Of course I do. So, who are my opponents?"

"Ah," said the older man, "That I cannot tell you. You will have to find out for yourself, Sire."

As Kameran said this, Gabriel frowned slightly, tightening his grip on the reins a little more. "Well then, wish me luck," he muttered under his breath.

As if hearing him, Sir Kameran stood at attention and bowed low to him. "Good luck, Your Majesty."

"Thank you," the young man replied. Slowly, Gabriel clamored up into the saddle with the help of Kameran and a stool built for the purpose, and adjusted himself until he felt as comfortable as possible, which wasn't much when you were wearing iron pants. The metal shifted in strange places, and being atop a horse didn't make it any easier. He sighed to himself and decided he would just have to deal with it. Then, easy and slow, he gave Solstice a gentle kick in the flanks, and directed the horse onto the field.

As his head met the golden glow of sunshine, a loud cheer erupted from the stands above him. He looked around, a little nervous, and saw that hundreds of people sat in the benches above him: men, women, and children alike. They had all come to see his match, and now the fear and anxiety was welling up in his chest. Just as he was about to turn around and go back the way he'd come, a hand reached out from beside him and took the reins, pulling him and Solstice farther into the arena. Gabriel shot a glance down to see who it belonged to, and frowned slightly as he saw a manservant with golden hair that matched the sun's rays. The servant didn't even look at him as they trotted further along the gravel path toward the middle of the field.

As they arrived, he noticed two people standing in the center of the arena. One was Sir Kameran, who glanced over at him and smiled kindly. *How did he get there so fast?* wondered Gabriel. The other was David Whittenburg, who was facing the crowd with a finger raised and his spectacles pushed all the way back. He looked like he was counting how many people were in the audience. As Gabriel and Solstice neared, however, he turned to face them both and smiled widely. Gabriel peered at the two men as Solstice came to a halt in front of them, pounding a hoof into the ground impatiently.

"Ah, you made it, Sire!" Whittenburg exclaimed in an excited tone, "The crowd has been eagerly awaiting your arrival." Kameran nodded in agreement, his silver armor glistening in the mid-morning sun. As confident and cheerful as both men were, Gabriel gave them both a nervous glance. Physical tests such as these were not his strong suit, but if it meant that he would become king sooner, then he had no other choice. Sighing to himself, he watched as Whittenburg made his way toward the crowd, raising his arms into the air to silence them.

"Greetings, ladies and gentlemen!" the elderly scholar announced loudly. "We are pleased to have you join us for such a momentous occasion. Now, without further ado, let the first match begin!" Cheers and claps arose from around the stands, echoing loudly through the stadium. At this, Gabriel stared at the crowd in amazement; so many people were expecting him to win, and the nervous feeling in the pit of his stomach returned even stronger than before. *Will I be able to do this?* he wondered.

Before he could think any further on the subject, the loud fanfare sounded again—this time from the other side of the arena, near the visitors' entrance. Everyone hushed and turned their attention toward the source of the sound, only to see another horse and rider making their way onto the field. As the rider approached, Gabriel glared, and his fingers clasped into fists. He knew who it was, and he wasn't impressed.

The silver-clad rider stopped in front of him, helmet visor up, sneering at him rudely.

"Greetings, cousin," Ayden said snidely, snickering under his breath. Gabriel's scowl hardened, but just as he was about to give Ayden a piece of his mind, Whittenburg stepped between their steeds and cleared his throat.

"Now listen, you two," Gabriel's adviser said, looking from one boy to another. "No funny business. No tricks or traps or outside help. This is a one-on-one fight, and I want it done properly." He then handed each of them a long lance that ended in a blunt, padded tip that would prevent injury. Both young men nodded, not taking their eyes off one another, though Ayden was still smirking. *What does he have planned?* Gabriel wondered, curiosity mixing with his aggression and apprehension.

Their intense gaze didn't last long; the two abruptly turned away from one another and walked their horses the length of the field to their designated positions. As Gabriel faced Solstice forward, he could see some of the faces of the spectators in the bleachers. A few looked worried, others showed excitement, and yet others simply sat and watched intently. He swallowed hard as he looked around at them all. Anxiety crept into his chest again, but he took a deep breath and settled himself down. Then, pushing the brown locks out of his eyes, he placed the heavy golden helmet atop his head.

He was as ready as he would ever be.

Just then, the sound of a loud bang echoed loudly through the arena, startling the horses slightly as it signaled for the match to begin. Gabriel gripped the long wooden lance tightly, then snapped the reins and gave his steed a quick but gentle kick in the flanks. Solstice reared onto his hind legs, nearly bucking Gabriel off his back, and then shot forward at a breakneck pace down the length of the arena toward their opponent. It felt incredible; the wind made Gabriel feel light as a feather, and though the lance was a bit awkward to carry, he was able to keep it steadily seated in the boot close to his waist. Rushing, running, faster and faster, bolting head-first toward his opponent, hoping to do him in: the excitement of the match elevated his spirits, and a wide, wild grin spread across his face.

The two steeds raced toward each other so fast that their stamping made the entire arena tremble in their wake. Just then, Gabriel noticed that his cousin's lance was tilted toward Solstice's chest plate. A gasp escaped Gabriel's lips; Ayden was trying to play dirty! They both knew that a horse's chest armor was the weakest part of the whole outfit, so that's where he was aiming first. At this, Gabriel's expression hardened and he gripped his weapon tighter. He wasn't going to let Ayden get that far.

Gabriel leaned forward to give himself a little more reach. As soon as Ayden was within reach of Gabriel's lance, the young monarch forcefully jabbed his weapon into his cousin's chest, catching Ayden off guard. He let out a loud grunt, both in surprise and due to the force of the blow, and his lance was jolted from his hands, missing Solstice completely. In an attempt to grab the weapon before it fell, Ayden let go of the reins of his own horse and slipped from the saddle, falling onto his side in the gravel.

As Ayden hit the dirt, another fanfare was heard, signaling the end of the match. Applause and loud cheers once again arose from the crowd, praising Gabriel as the winner. Ayden, short of breath and sweating profusely, was firmly escorted from the field after much cursing. Coming to a stop in the middle of the arena, Gabriel slid the hot and heavy helmet from his mahogany head and looked up at the audience, a sense of pride welling up in his chest and a smile forming on his lips. He had won; he had actually won his first match! *If only Reggie could see me now*, he thought.

However, just as he'd gotten used to the sense of pride and the excitement, another loud trumpeting was heard. Gabriel readjusted himself in the saddle, peering at the gate on the other side of the field. Who would it be this time? The butcher? The blacksmith? Sir Kameran? Immediately, everyone hushed once again and turned to the visitors' entrance to see who the next opponent would be.

CHAPTER 9

IT'S JOUST A GAME!
(PART 2)

A hush fell over the crowd as the rider appeared through the visitor's entrance. Then the second opponent made his way onto the field, and as his fiery-red hair came into view, Gabriel's jaw dropped open in surprise. Coming across the arena toward them was a young man he knew all too well, and one that he definitely had *not* expected to be his opponent in this competition. With a grin, the redhead came to a stop next to him.

"Arthur?" Gabriel blurted, "What are you doing here?"

"What's it look like? We're competing!" came Arthur's hearty response, silver armor gleaming in the mid-morning sun as though it had just been polished. Gabriel just stared at his friend in astonishment. What was he thinking? How could he do this? The very idea of going head-to-head with someone he was so close to made his stomach churn, his armored fingers curling around his twisting abdomen. Arthur looked like he wasn't worried about the match at all. He didn't even seem to notice Gabriel's unease and turned back around, gathering up a lance and walking his steed, a brown stallion not much smaller than Gabriel's, to their starting point.

Gabriel watched him move away slowly as Arthur waved to an applauding crowd, and then the young king turned Solstice around, making his way to the other side of the field. His mind was still clouded with worries: what was going to happen? What if Arthur were to lose? Would he hate Gabriel? What if Gabriel didn't have the heart to defeat his best friend, and he let Arthur win? He would lose all his followers and his rights to the throne. Sighing heavily, he hung his head slightly and continued on. Just then, Whittenburg, who had been watching from a fair distance, appeared next to Gabriel, patting his gold-clad leg.

"Good show, Sire!" he said cheerfully. "That last match was excellent. Now you must defeat Arthur, then one more opponent, and then the task will be done. I know you can do it, Sire." With another reassuring pat on the leg, his adviser turned and walked away, leaving the young men facing each other. They stared at one another for a few moments. This was it. Gabriel had to make a difficult decision: to let his friend win the match and lose the respect he had worked so hard to obtain, or to take the victory himself and assure his title and position, at the risk of Arthur's friendship. As Gabriel peered at his comrade, he could see a look of determination in Arthur's eyes, and knew that the match at hand would not be an easy one.

As the boys stared at each other, awaiting the signal to start, the stadium fell silent. Slowly, he slid the heavy gold helm over his head once again. Now that the sun had risen more, the armor was hotter and heavier than ever, making it even harder to maneuver in. Gabriel glanced up at Arthur, wondering what his best buddy was thinking at that moment.

Once again, a loud bang resounded through the arena, and down came their lances as the boys kicked their steeds into motion, tilting at full tilt toward each other. The air around them buzzed with tension, but this time, Gabriel kept his composure, holding the lance tightly to his side. As they neared each other, Gabriel noticed Arthur's lance pointed directly at his own chest plate; the very same thing he himself had done to Ayden. Instinctively he raised his own weapon to ward off the strike, successfully doing so. Arthur's weapon slid against his, not fully upright, and the boys passed each other without a scratch. They came to a halt a few yards away from each other, then turned to face one another. Once they had readjusted themselves, they snapped the reins and repeated the same action, charging full force toward each other.

This went on for a good fifteen minutes. By then, both the boys and the horses were tired and hot. The metal armor made it nearly impossible to breathe, and Gabriel barely had the strength to take up his weapon once more. This time, he had to do it; he had to defeat Arthur, no matter the cost. Sweat rolled down his face behind the gleaming helm, but he fixed himself once more and held the lance at the ready. Breathing hard, he gently kicked Solstice's sides, and the stallion reared once again, then bolted as fast as he could muster toward Arthur and his horse. Arthur was barely seated properly in the saddle, but Gabriel had to gather as much strength as he could to keep the lance at hip level at the least. As he neared his opponent, he could see that Arthur was struggling as well. *This is it*, he thought, *this is my chance.* He lifted his weapon a little higher and jabbed it at Arthur's chest. Arthur wasn't prepared, or aware enough, to parry the blow, and took the brunt of the hit, allowing himself to be knocked off the horse. He fell to the ground with a loud grunt, while his horse came to a complete stop. The whole arena let out a gasp.

Gabriel turned back and watched his friend fall, half-proud of himself for winning once again, but half-horrified at the possibility of his comrade getting hurt. He faced the horse toward Arthur and began to trot Solstice back toward him, hoping he wasn't injured too badly. As he came closer, he could hear the crowd in the stands begin to clap and cheer. They didn't see two best friends fighting for a kingship. They saw one opponent defeat another; they saw their future king excel and move on to the next stage of the match. Soon, Gabriel came to a stop by his friend's side and reached down to help him up, an apologetic look in his eyes. His friend stood up with difficulty and took his helmet off, a smile spreading across Arthur's face.

"Well done, Gabe," his companion said to the astonished young king, pushing aside the curls of ginger hair clinging to his forehead from perspiration. Gabriel removed his own helm and stared at Arthur.

"Arthur..." he started, dismounting his steed with some trouble, "Why? Why did you enter the match?"

Arthur shrugged, wincing as he placed an armored hand to his upper chest. "They needed someone to be your opponent, so I volunteered. Plus, I thought it would be fun."

"But you could have gotten hurt..."

"It was a risk I was willing to take, Gabe," Arthur replied with a small wink. Gabriel only shook his head. Arthur was then ushered off the field, while Gabriel and Solstice were escorted off to the other side of the arena, where Sir Kameran was waiting for him with a canteen of cool water.

"Good show, Sire," the tired knight said with a genuine smile as Gabriel drank. As he lowered the canteen, Gabriel gave him a confused look.

"What's going on, Kameran?"

"We're going to give you a small break for now, Sire, so you can cool off and recharge for your last match," Sir Kameran explained calmly, "So let's get your armor off, then you and Solstice can have a rest." Gabriel nodded in agreement and followed Kameran to the stables to get his armor removed, leading his weary horse.

Two stable lads were waiting. They took Solstice's reins from Gabriel, leading him down the hay-littered hall and into a nice, warm stall that had been freshly mucked out and remade with new straw. Then Gabriel was ushered to the bench where he had put his armor on and, with a little help, removed the hot, bulky metal protection. As he took off his chest plate and gauntlets, he could see large, dark stains upon his shirt from where he had perspired freely. Under his arms and around his neck, he was dripping with sweat. Once his greaves had dropped, he slid down onto the wooden bench and let out a harsh sigh. Wiping his brow, he looked up and about the stables as a hand pressed a flagon of sugary water into his hand. The servants were all rushing about, preparing for the third and final match. He wondered who his opponent would be as he sipped the water; the coolness of it made him feel better. Perhaps it would be the blacksmith after all; he was good with all sorts of weapons. Or maybe it would be Sir Kameran, since he was the Captain of the Knights and a seasoned warrior. The more he thought about it, the more worried he felt, and he swallowed hard, trying to make the lump in his throat recede. Not even a deep draft of water could help with that, though.

A pleasant breeze blew through the stables, and Gabriel let out another, calmer sigh. He wiped away another bead of sweat and stood up, taking a small stroll down the long path toward the entrance of the arena. Peering into the stands, he could see the townsfolk talking excitedly amongst themselves, and he also spied some of the Elder Council seated in one of the highest stands, giving each other looks of interest. The knot formed in his stomach again. He disliked them, with their beady gazes and sneering faces. They never seemed to be happy or impressed, their faces frozen in permanent scowls. Though he was still nervous, Gabriel turned back into the hallway and strode back to the stables.

As he entered the stable again, warmth soaked into his tired aching body. He stretched a little, twisting his torso to the left and right. Once he felt he was ready to go, he walked back to the bench where his armor awaited him. The same stable lad helped him into the chest piece and the greaves, being careful not to adjust them too tightly. The cowters and vambraces he handled himself. Then, Gabriel slipped the gauntlets on, and the servant helped him into the saddle once Solstice had been brought out. Gabriel nodded, satisfied with how he felt, and once again he gave Solstice a small kick, ushering the horse forward toward the stadium entrance.

A roar of applause and cheering sounded as he entered the field. Some of the townsfolk even rose from their seats, smiling and clapping for their king. This made Gabriel smile, though he still felt the tight nervous feeling in his chest. Across the field, just as Gabriel and Solstice reached the middle of the arena, another rider entered the field. As this new opponent neared the center of the field, the stands fell deathly silent. Clad in silver armor, his new adversary wore a shining helmet that completely covered his head, hiding his face. This made Gabriel's nerves tremble even more. *So I'm not going to find out who this opponent is...* he thought, shifting in the saddle uneasily. All he could tell was that this opponent was smaller than the others, wiry rather than muscular. The two opponents faced each other, their steeds stamping their hooves anxiously a couple of times. A gentle wind blew between them, but the competitors stayed silent. Just then, Whittenburg walked up to them.

"All right, you two, this is the last match," he started, "No foul play, and good luck to you both." The silver rider just nodded in acknowledgment, as did Gabriel, and the two of them turned and walked to their own sides of the arena. The tension in the air was so thick you could have cut it with a butter knife. As he passed by, Gabriel stole a glance up at the stands, hoping to see a happy or cheering face; but all he could see were looks of anxiety and tense stares. He sighed once again, then slipped his helmet down over his head, sweat still staining the inside of it. *This is it,* he thought to himself, *After this, I only have one more trial...* Nervousness was eating away at the pit of his stomach. Was he really ready for this?

He didn't have much time to think about it as he reached his position. Slowly he turned and faced his opponent, taking the lance from the servant who handed it to him. He continued to wonder just who this person was; he had the metal visor of the helmet down, so no one could see his face. Not even a hair showed under the helm. As he pondered the possibilities, Gabriel became more tense and nervous.

Just then, there came another loud bang, and the horses whinnied and reared as they had before. They then jolted into action, hurtling at top speed toward each other. Gabriel felt every lurch forward, his already-hot armor shifting against his body. The lance at his side seemed much heavier than when he had first started, but he held on as tightly as he could, determined not to lose. The horses drew nearer, and just as the royal youth was about to thrust his weapon at the other rider, their lances collided, allowing them to pass by each other unscathed. Neither had been hurt, and neither had lost his weapon. As quickly as he could, Gabriel turned Solstice about-face and righted himself to the best of his ability, noticing his opponent doing the same. The other rider didn't seem fazed at all; not being able to see his facial expressions was making it hard for Gabriel to predict just how far he would be able to go. Deciding not to hold back, he charged at the rider once again.

Blow after blow rained down, neither of the opponents giving an inch to the other. The silver-armored rider matched Gabriel's thrusts and stabs perfectly, deflecting them with ease. Gabriel could feel himself getting tired, and his muscles ached, but he knew he couldn't give up; he *wouldn't* give up. His determination kept him going, and finally, after what seemed like half an hour, he managed to land a hit on the mystery rider. The other rider must have been worn out as well, for as Gabriel jabbed at the silver chest plate one final time, the rider failed to raise the lance high enough to block his attack. The lance shot forward, and hit the other rider in the chest with a loud, hard *CLANG*. The rider couldn't withstand the force behind the blow, and he fell from the horse to the gravel below, landing on his back.

Applause and cheers once again rose from the stands behind him. He had done it! He had won! He had passed the test and had kept his entitlement to kingship! As he slid the helmet off his head, a wide grin upon his face, Gabriel looked around at the townspeople. They were all cheering for him, even the Elder Council. He looked down toward where his opponent had fallen, and his grin quickly faded. Peeking out from under the silver helm were a few stray locks of pale yellow hair, of a color he knew very well. Fear began to creep up in his chest, and he slid out of his saddle roughly as the rider raised his head, the hot, heavy helmet sliding off completely. As they saw who it was, everyone in the stadium gasped loudly, even Gabriel; long golden hair cascaded down the rider's clad back, and those green eyes were unmistakable.

"Caitlin...?" Gabriel uttered in shock.

The blonde silver-clad girl rubbed her messy hair, looking up at Gabriel with a sheepish grin. "You're better than I thought, Gabe," she commented in a slightly wheezy tone. The lance must have hit her harder than he'd thought. His eyes drooped as he gave her a concerned look.

"What were you thinking? You could have been seriously hurt!" Gabriel replied sharply, reaching out his armored hand to help her up. She seemed slightly winded, but took his hand and stood up weakly.

"I know..." she started, looking away from him with a disheartened expression, "But they needed another opponent for you, and I wanted to show everyone that girls can fight, too." She twisted her foot into the ground in embarrassment. Gabriel knew he couldn't stay mad at her for long, and only shook his head. Before he could say more, the two of them were separated, and Whittenburg stepped up to him with a wide smile on his face.

"Well done, Sire! You have passed your first physical trial," he said with a cheerful voice, but Gabriel didn't feel happy about it. He was worried about his friends; what if they were seriously injured? He wouldn't be able to live with himself if they couldn't forgive him.

Whittenburg didn't seem to notice Gabriel's somber expression, and turned to their audience, addressing them. "This concludes today's event! Thank you all for joining us! We will be having a feast tonight to celebrate our new king's victory, and we hope you all will attend!" Having finished, he turned back to Gabriel, who watched as the townsfolk filed out of the stadium slowly, excited looks on their faces. They were chatting happily amongst themselves, seeming genuinely impressed with their king's performance. Gabriel turned to his steed, taking the reins and patting his head, at which the horse nudged him fondly. "You did it, Solstice," he cooed to the animal, who only snorted his reply and rubbed his head against Gabriel's cheek in admiration.

"Sire, I must say, you have a knack for jousting. Well done," came Whittenburg's voice behind him, which made Gabriel stop in his tracks.

He turned to his mentor slowly, but did not meet his gaze. "Yeah, I guess so..."

"Why, Your Majesty, whatever is the matter?" the old man said, his eyes portraying worry. Gabriel only sighed and averted his own eyes further.

"It doesn't feel right. Arthur and Caitlin could have been hurt much worse than they are," He began to turn around to lead his steed off toward the stable when Whittenburg placed his hand on the youth's shoulder, making him stop and look up at his mentor.

"I think you'll find that your friends are a little more forgiving than you think," he said gently, giving Gabriel's shoulder a soft squeeze, "Come, Sire, let's let your trusty steed rest. I'm sure you need to as well." Gabriel just nodded and allowed himself to be led away, off the turf and toward the stable entrance. Once inside, the familiar aromas and the warmth of the stables wafted by them, easing his aching muscles and bringing a smile to his face. He sighed a little and Solstice snorted quietly, leaning his head down to munch on the straw scattered across the ground. Whittenburg ushered the two of them further in, and a stable hand took Solstice's reins and pulled him toward his stall. The stable hands applauded Gabriel as he walked through, smiling and bowing, acknowledging his victory.

As he walked back to the bench where he had donned his armor, Gabriel let out a heavy sigh and pulled the hot, sweaty helm from his head, letting it clatter to the floor. He did the same with the gauntlets, vambraces, cowters, and greaves, shaking them off as he walked. Whittenburg had to step aside to avoid being hit or tripping over Gabriel's shed armor. As he reached the bench, sweat pouring from his face and arms, he unfastened the breastplate as fast as he could and slid it to the ground, dropping to the wooden seat with a loud grunt as his head hung tiredly. He sat there for a couple minutes, just breathing slowly, trying to calm his pounding heart.

Once he had cooled off a bit, he stood and followed Whittenburg out through the doorway toward the entrance, waving goodbye to Solstice before he left. As they walked, he rubbed his sore arms and legs, and placed a hand on the back of his neck, stretching as much as he could. Riding was strenuous enough; it was much worse when you had to wear armor and hold a large, heavy weapon. It was killer on the joints.

Gabriel let out another heavy breath, and looked up to see his comrades coming from the other direction. Neither Caitlin nor Arthur looked hurt; in fact, they were laughing and smiling, as though nothing had happened. Curious but happy, Gabriel called out to them and waved. Both looked up at the sound of their names and grinned, rushing to his side and embracing him tightly, as he winced due to his soreness. "Wow, that was an awesome match, Gabe!" Arthur blurted out as he pulled away from the group. Caitlin pulled back as well. Both had changed back into civilian attire, but Gabriel hadn't, and his clothing was still drenched in sweat.

"Yeah, it was. Thanks for everything, guys," he commented in a weary voice.

"Aw, we knew you could do it, Gabe," Caitlin answered, grinning and waving her hand nonchalantly. "It just took a little challenge to bring it out."

"Well, I don't know about you guys, but all that riding has worked up my appetite," Gabriel announced. "Let's go eat!"

All four of them turned and walked back toward the castle, where a feast fit for a king awaited them.

CHAPTER 10

RESPITE

That night's feast had been a great success, and had pulled in quite the crowd. Gabriel reminded himself that he needed to thank the cooks and chefs for their hard work. After the feast was over, Gabriel conversed with many people, talking over the last few trials and what he might have in store for him in the near future.

Finally, once all the guests had returned to their homes and inns, Gabriel went to his bedchamber, flopping tiredly onto the feather mattress. He didn't even bother to take off the clean clothing that he'd changed into before dinner, and fell fast asleep beneath the covers of his four-poster bed. The crickets chirped merrily outside his window, and the moon's glow brightened the night sky as lights around the town square and in the castle dimmed and disappeared. It was a rather quiet night for the residents of Halcyon Ridge.

The next morning, sunlight spread across the valley and through the town as the sun rose. Everything went as it normally would; shops opened as the sun peeped over the horizon, with the shopkeepers placing their wares upon shelves and pedestals, and of course the bakers and gardeners were up extra early to make sure the breads and flowers looked and smelled their best. The tired knights from the night before were replaced with rested soldiers who were ready to take on the day. The sun crept upward along its celestial path, stretching its warm rays along the castle walls, illuminating the gray stones and climbing ivy with a golden glow.

Soon its light filtered in through the cracked shudders of Gabriel's bedroom, but he was already awake, lying in bed and staring up at the ceiling with his arms folded behind his head. He had stripped off his clothing from the night before, and was deep in thought, pondering his previous tests—especially the fact that in the last trial, he could have hurt his friends terribly if he hadn't been careful. He also wondered if Reggie had been through the same type of trials as he had, and if his older brother would be proud of him for what he had accomplished.

There came soft knock at the door. It wasn't loud, but it was enough to jolt Gabriel out of his daydreaming and cause him to rise from the warm sheets. Quickly, he raced to his closet to search for suitable clothing. He threw on a plain, light brown button-up shirt, then rapidly replaced his undergarments and pulled on a pair of maroon pants and a clean pair of wool socks. He heard another soft knock just as he was reaching for his boots and called out to the person behind the door, "Just a minute! I'll be right there!"

"Your Maj– um, Gabriel... it's Ashlyn," came a quiet response from behind the wood. The voice shocked him a little, because he was surprised that she would be at his door, especially this early in the morning. He finally finished slipping the calf-high boots onto his feet and strode slowly to the door, opening it warily. There stood the girl he had secretly fallen for, golden hair and bright green eyes shining.

He smiled. "Ashlyn, what are you doing here?" he asked, and a shy smile spread across her lips as she diverted her gaze toward the floor.

"I-I wanted to be the first to greet you today," she replied timidly, pulling at the hem of her dress.

Gabriel bowed to her, which caused her cheeks to turn pink. "Then, good morning, Miss," he responded in the most regal tone he could muster, making his visitor giggle a bit. She, in turn, lowered herself and raised an edge of her skirt, curtsying to him.

"And a good morning to you, Your Highness," she shot back, causing them both to laugh out loud. Their voices carried down the granite stairwell behind Ashlyn, making the dreary hall seem brighter.

"Would you like to come and get some breakfast with me?" Gabriel asked impulsively.

"That sounds wonderful, Sire." Without another word, they began to walk down the long staircase together toward the kitchen.

The tapping of their shoes resounded against the old stones under them as they descended and crossed the great hall. Subconsciously, their hands had linked themselves, making the castle staff who saw them smile and chuckle fondly. The two had no idea why until they entered the large dining hall, where members to the Council and other VIPs sat for their morning meal. It was there that Gabriel turned to Ashlyn and looked at their hands, his cheeks flushing a light pink as he released her.

"Good morning, Your Highness," chorused several voices from his left, and as Gabriel turned, he could see his friends sitting at the long wooden table, waving to him as they ate. "Did you sleep well, Sire?" David Whittenburg asked, pushing his spectacles higher on his crooked nose. Beside him were Caitlin's father, Sir Kameran, and Arthur's mother, Matron Winter. They both smiled courteously and bowed their heads in respect.

Gabriel bowed in return and turned to his adviser. "I did, Lord Whittenburg, thank you," he replied, then turned to Ashlyn, who had been cowering slightly behind him, now looking nervous and anxious. "I also brought a guest with me for breakfast."

"Splendid!" cried Matron Winter, who walked up to the timid girl and took her hay-scratched hands. "So nice to see one of the stable girls for once."

"What do you mean?" Sir Kameran retorted. "I see her all the time on my way to the armory." The head knight wiped his mouth with a napkin, his scruffy beard still stained with egg yolk. Gabriel then noticed something odd about his friend's father, more particularly about his attire; Kameran wasn't wearing any armor! Kameran must have seen and understood the strange look that Gabriel gave him, as he laughed and peered down at himself. "I forget that Your Majesty doesn't see me in civilian clothing often. My apologies."

"No, no, it's all right, Sir Kameran," Gabriel responded quickly, "It's nice to know that there's a real person under all that metal." At this, all three adults burst into hearty laughter.

Gabriel looked to his guest, realizing finally that she was staring hungrily at the table laid with food. "Hey, let's go find a seat, Ash," he said softly, gently grasping her hand in his once again. The straw-haired girl followed him, and they took their places by Gabriel's best friends.

"Good morning, Gabe and Ash!" Caitlin said excitedly, sitting in her seat like a proper lady.

"M-Hey, guys!" Arthur muffled through a large bite of food, making Caitlin turn to him and scowl hard, with her hands on her hips.

"Arthur! Didn't your mother ever tell you not to talk with your mouth full?" she snapped.

Arthur swallowed whatever he had in his mouth and shot an annoyed glance right back at her. "Well, you certainly aren't my mum, so quit it, will ya?"

"Knock it off, you two," Gabriel stated with a small laugh, amused by his comrades, "It's great to see you too."

"Come, come, sit down and eat something," Caitlin ushered, pulling out the chair to her left. Ashlyn timidly sat down beside the other blonde girl, seemingly unsure if it was all right for her to be sitting next to one of the future king's friends. Gabriel sat himself down on Arthur's right side, and no sooner had they settled in than their food was brought out to them; eggs over easy with shredded potatoes in the Irish boxty style. All of it made Gabriel's mouth water, and he immediately began to shovel the delicious meal into his mouth, just as Arthur had.

Ashlyn looked down at her meal as it was placed in front of her. Tentatively, she picked up the fork closest to her, looking very unsure of herself. Gabriel noticed this from the corner of his eye and watched her carefully, while still munching away on his own breakfast. She probably wasn't used to eating anywhere but in servant's quarters; being among friends with fancy silverware and new experiences must be hard for her to get used to. Gabriel continued to peer at her as she slowly lifted the utensil to the plate, gently stabbed a fluffy piece of egg, and raised it to her lips. The whole time, her tiny hand was shaking slightly; it was obvious that she was nervous. The food then entered her mouth, and her whole face lit up. "Wow..." Ashlyn murmured through her mouthful, making Gabriel beam slightly.

"How is it?" came Caitlin's voice from her right.

The stable girl finished chewing and swallowing, then looked at her new friend and smiled. "It's delicious," she responded happily, taking another bite with no hesitation. With a grin, Caitlin went back to her own food. After that, the four friends continued to sit together and eat, sometimes greeting others, but mostly talking amongst themselves. They told Ashlyn about all of the adventures they'd been on when they were younger, and how much they all despised Ayden. The more they spoke with one another, the more Ashlyn opened up; she talked more, she laughed more. It made Gabriel smile to know that she was happier now that she was among friends.

Meanwhile, a lone figure stood in the shadows, peering in disgust at the comrades; how could they eat together with the common folk, pretending all was sweetness and light? He glared at them with a piercing pair of dark brown eyes for a few more moments, then turned away from the dining room and hurried down the hall.

After the four had finished their meal, they thanked the servants and excused themselves from the room. Just outside the doorway in the entrance hall stood Lord Whittenburg, speaking to a small group of aristocrats, the expression on his face one of stoic calmness. Gabriel and his friends slipped by them undetected and walked to the entrance door of the castle proper, pushing it open. The door was heavy, but with all four of them pushing, it opened with ease. As they stepped into the cool crisp morning, a calm gentle breeze brushed by them.

A sigh escaped from Gabriel's lips as he smiled and looked out upon the courtyard. Caitlin and Arthur followed suit and also exhaled happily, standing side by side with their royal friend. The castle staff were hard at work trimming hedges and watering flowers, feeding animals and tending to the vegetable, fruit, and flower gardens. It was a sight to behold.

"So," Arthur asked, "What do you want to do today, Gabe?"

Gabriel put a hand on his chin in thought. "Hmm... I don't know," he responded truthfully, "I haven't had a day off in a while."

"W-Well..." came Ashlyn's soft voice behind them, which made them all turn to her in unison, "The day is young. We could go for a trail ride with the horses, or go swimming at a lake..." Gabriel noticed a hint of pink blush on her cheeks as she said this, but he looked to his friends, who were nodding and smiling. Gabriel himself grinned as well, and turned back to the straw-haired stable girl.

"Sounds like a great idea, Ash."

Ashlyn's face turned even redder as a surprised look spread across it. "I-It does?"

"Yeah," agreed Caitlin. "I haven't taken Starlight out for a ride in a long time. I bet she would love it." Arthur nodded in approval, and as Ashlyn looked at them in turn, she smiled brightly, her jade eyes aglow with excitement.

Gabriel put his hands on his hips and grinned, looking at the three of them. "Then it's settled! A trail ride and a swimming trip it is!" he exclaimed, and the others cheered happily in agreement. "Now, everyone go grab your things, then we'll meet up back at the stables as soon as possible. Don't forget to let an adult know where you're going so they won't be worried about us the entire time."

All three of his friends stood at attention and saluted him. "Aye, aye, sir!" they proclaimed together, then, as they giggled and chuckled, scattered in different directions. Gabriel hurried inside to grab his things. On the way, however, he was stopped by Whittenburg, who had completed his meeting with the aristocrats.

"Oh my, where are you off to in such a hurry, Sire?"

"Ashlyn, Caitlin, Arthur and I are all going on a trail ride today, so I'm off to get my riding boots and some supplies—"

"Now hold on," Whittenburg interrupted, frowning. "Who is going with you as a guard?"

"A guard?" Gabriel echoed, puzzled.

Whittenburg pushed his glasses further onto his nose. "Why yes, Sire," he stated in a matter-of-fact tone. "You must start thinking of these things! You will need at least one bodyguard if you want to go anywhere outside the city gates. You are our king, after all. We wouldn't want anything bad to happen to you!"

Gabriel rolled his eyes. He knew that becoming king was going to be a big responsibility, but he hadn't thought that he was going to need a babysitter wherever he went. *How annoying...* However, at that moment, his mind wandered to his brother. Reggie had always had a knight stationed at his side, even as he slept. Being king of the realm was a dangerous business, after all; there were those who would happily take the realm, or his life, away from him... and even guarded on the battlefield, he had still disappeared last month. Sighing, Gabriel turned back to his adviser. "All right, David, I'll take a guard with me. But can I choose my own?"

"Of course, Sire. Whom do you wish to take with you?"

"Sir Kameran, if I may."

"Very well," Whittenburg answered with a small bow, "I will inform him immediately." He took his leave, while Gabriel raced toward his bedchamber.

Later, once everyone had donned their riding gear and equipped themselves with an extra change of clothing, they met inside the barn, accompanied by Sir Kameran. At first, Caitlin was opposed to having her father tagging along, but once Gabriel explained the reason for his presence, she just nodded and smiled, understanding his motives. Everyone had decided to wear light-brown riding pants and high leather riding boots, and they all carried with them padded riding helmets adorned with velvety black cloth. Ashlyn wore a long-sleeved dark blue blouse which she had borrowed from Caitlin, who was wearing a dark green blouse of the same type. The boys were all wearing short-sleeved shirts, Gabriel in red and Arthur in green, while Sir Kameran was wearing the same half-armor suit he had worn in the dining hall that morning; a chest plate, black riding gloves, and armored boots. At his side rested a gleaming silver sword in a decorated scabbard; a useful tool and deadly weapon, should the need arise.

They walked deeper into the stables, where their steeds waited patiently. They each greeted their horses, then proceeded to mount. *It's a lot easier without the armor,* Gabriel thought. The only one to have any trouble was Ashlyn, who seem unaccustomed to riding a horse. Gabriel noticed her quivering hands as she held the reins, and he reached over to calm her. "Hey, you'll do fine, okay? We'll be right here to help you," he said softly.

Ashlyn's cheeks flushed, and she nodded to him firmly. "Thank you, Sire—Gabriel," she replied nervously. Smiling, Gabriel gave Solstice a gentle kick, and with a loud snort, the massive animal began to prance forward. The others followed.

The five of them rode through the town square in single file, greeting the townsfolk as they passed. Most of the people they saw stared in awe, smiling at the small troop, while others cheered happily or wished them well. Gabriel was happy to be getting some fresh air and a little break from his duties as the next ruler of his kingdom; it could get really stuffy being stuck in the castle all day long. When they finally reached the town gates, the soldiers guarding it stopped them, asking for their reasons for leaving. Sir Kameran took the lead and explained everything, and the two guards nodded, wishing the group a safe journey. Then, chatting cheerfully, the five riders passed through the gate and continued on their way to their new adventure.

Once outside the gate, Gabriel looked about the thick, lush forest the town was nestled within; trees and bushes lined the path before them, and stretched as far as he could see. The trail led them, in time, down into a large, rather dismal valley, where Gabriel knew that the battle in which his brother had vanished a few months prior had taken place. He had no idea it was so close to home… Would he actually get to see the site where his brother had, presumably, perished?

A knot formed in his abdomen as he thought about this, but his mind didn't linger on it long. A moment later, he heard Ashlyn speak up. "Look over there, guys!" she cried excitedly as she pointed to what looked like a gravel road that led deeper into the woods.

"Will that take us to the lake?" Arthur asked.

"I believe so," Sir Kameran answered. "If we take this route, we'll eventually end up coming out near the castle as well. It loops around."

"Well, what are we waiting for? Let's go!" exclaimed Caitlin, pulling the reins hard and turning her white mare toward the path, galloping ahead of them. Arthur laughed loudly and followed suit, snapping his chocolate-colored stallion into action and following the bubbly blonde into the mouth of the leafy path.

Kameran smiled and chuckled. "Oh, that daughter of mine... " he said, shaking his head a little, then turning to Gabriel and Ashlyn. "Come on, you two, we don't want to be left behind." They hustled toward the leafy trail as well, with Kameran bringing up the rear.

The trail was more overgrown than it looked, with tall trees and fuller underbrush, the sun's light barely able to filter through the canopy above them. The only sounds Gabriel heard apart from their breathing was the continuous crackle of twigs snapping under the horses' hooves, and the soft chirping of the birds in the tall hardwoods. The absence of all other noise made the woods around them eerily quiet, but Gabriel didn't mind at all. In fact, he smiled and closed his eyes for a few moments, bowing his head in thought. The calmness of the area cooled his nerves and anxieties, making his worries slip from his shoulders for a while, leaving him feeling peaceful. The stillness of the forest was enough to calm even the most troubled mind, he imagined, which was probably why Ashlyn had suggested that they come here.

Gabriel then looked over at the young lady beside him, who was watching the path ahead of them intently. "Ashlyn, are you well?" he asked, concern in his voice. She jumped a little and turned, blushing a slight pink as she did.

"Y-Yes, I'm all right," she replied, turning back to the gravel road, "I'm... Just not used to riding, that's all."

Gabriel gave her a reassuring smile and nodded. "You'll get the hang of it," he replied softly, then turned his eyes forward. They could barely see Caitlin and Arthur, who had run off way ahead of them.

"The lake is just ahead," Sir Kameran stated, pointing a gloved hand toward their destination, "Come on." He then snapped the reins and rushed ahead of them, and Gabriel and Ashlyn followed suit, racing to keep up with him.

Soon they arrived at the lake, a beautiful spread of water surrounded by a small sandy beach and lush grass. It was a sight to behold indeed, and the water was crystal clear. Caitlin and Arthur had already changed into their swimming attire; Caitlin in a brown romper-type shirt and thigh-length pants, and Arthur in a light shirt and two pairs of shorts. Both waved to the small troop as they arrived and beckoned them to come into the water. Smiling, Gabriel grabbed his own two pairs of shorts and hid behind a tree, changing as quickly as he could. Then, he raced out to the water, jumping into the cool refreshing stillness. Not long after he had jumped, Caitlin and Arthur also dove in, making a huge splash as they did. Ashlyn was the last to join; wearing a dark maroon outfit, she eased herself into the water, shivering slightly at the coolness. Sir Kameran stood on the shore with their things, smirking as Gabriel hurried over to her and helped her into the water.

She smiled, nodding to him and blushing as always. Soon they were all having fun and splashing around like fish, cooling off in the refreshing water of the lake while Kameran stood guard.

It was late in the afternoon by the time they'd finished playing. The sun was preparing to set, and they were all getting hungry; it had been a long time since lunch. They climbed out of the water one at a time and hid in the trees to change into clean, dry clothing, then packed everything they had brought with them into their saddlebags and climbed atop their horses, who were cool and refreshed from having drunk the clear lake water. Once they had readied themselves, the ever-vigilant Sir Kameran took the helm once more, leading their small group out of the forest along the side trail that would bring them back to the castle. All the while, the four friends chatted like songbirds about the day's events. Sir

Kameran looked back at them, smiling, then faced forward again, not saying a word. This was a day to remember, one to bring out whenever his heart needed a little joy.

Gabriel looked at his friends, quiet now, as they continued to chat without him. He smiled, knowing that they had all had a good time; but now, sadly, the day was coming to an end, and he was no closer to being any less worried about the upcoming trial. His head hung low as he heard the sound of hooves approaching his side, and he looked up as Ashlyn pulled up beside him. She peered at him anxiously. "Is everything all right, Gabriel?" she asked, to which he just smiled and nodded, turning back to keep an eye on Sir Kameran.

"Yeah, I'm okay," he stated. "I'm just sad that the day is over already. It was fun."

Ashlyn let out a small giggle at his comment. "The day may be over, but we'll remember it for the rest of our days!" she replied with a smile, patting his shoulder fondly. Gabriel looked up at her and grinned. She was right; it was a day they would never forget.

Before long, Sir Kameran brought them into a little clearing, where up ahead they could see a narrow path that led out into the open area outside the town gates. "Almost home!" cried Caitlin. The others cheered in agreement, while the tired knight simply chuckled at their antics.

"Come, children, let's go home," he responded in a fatherly tone, giving his horse, Aztec, a nudge with his knees. The warhorse snorted a little, then led them out of the thick forest. He didn't require any guidance; he could smell the clean hay of home from here.

The light had started to fade behind the towers of the castle by the time they arrived at the keep, leaving a soft orange glow to light their way home. Gabriel smiled broadly and replayed that day's events in his mind; the warm welcome from Ashlyn, followed by the breakfast with his amazing friends, and then the wonderful, refreshing trip to the lake, accompanied with a calming trail ride. He couldn't have asked for a better day off. All of it had been a well-deserved break from the normal, mundane life of being royal. Not to mention, not having to try not to kill himself over the physical trials was always nice as well.

Sighing happily to himself, he trailed behind the group as they entered the town square, where shopkeepers were just beginning to close up for the night, and then as they rode into the stables, where Ashlyn said goodbye to them all and wished them well. The four others headed up to the castle for a well-rounded dinner.

CHAPTER 11

GET TO THE POINT
(PART 1)

"What a day..." Gabriel's voice echoed through his quiet bedchamber after he woke the next day. It was still quite early; there was hardly a sound as his feet gently pressed against the hardwood floor beneath him. Sleepily, he rubbed the gunk from his eyes and yawned loudly. He could only imagine what would be in store for him this time, and he reluctantly removed himself from his bed, tossing the covers aside lazily. He hoped it was fencing-related. He was actually pretty good with a rapier, less so with a broadsword. The final physical trial was to take place after breakfast, in the throne room, but his nerves had woken him earlier than he had meant to be awake. Sighing to himself, he slowly went to his closet, his feet scuffing softly across the floorboards. He pulled out a dark navy shirt and a pair of rich brown pants that matched his hair, slipped into them quickly and quietly, then pulled on his favorite boots. Satisfied with his outfit, he left the room silently.

After making sure the door was securely locked behind him, Gabriel descended the long, stony staircase toward the entrance hall. *Place could use a little decorating*, he thought. Maybe after the coronation, he could get the old goats on the Council to shake loose a little gold to put some tapestries or portraits or something on the dreary walls of the tower. Halcyon Ridge was known for its portrait artists; might as well celebrate them.

As he looked through the windows, he could see that the sun was barely beginning to peek over the horizon. He rubbed his eyes and yawned again as he saw a few knights walking up the steps toward him. It was the nightly patrol, doing their last rounds of the night; and as they noticed their future king, they bowed their heads in respect. Gabriel returned the gesture lazily, then the patrol continued on up the tall staircase as he finished his descent, then turned to make his way toward the kitchen. He knew that no one would be in the dining hall at the moment, for most of the castle was still sleeping; so he decided that he'd get a bite to eat from the source while he waited for everyone else.

Soon his nose picked up the delicious aromas of fried potatoes and sizzling bacon, causing his mouth to water. Smiling, Gabriel walked at a brisker pace. However, as he neared the kitchen area, he noticed that someone was ahead of him; a dark shadow among the lights of the lanterns on the walls. Gabriel hid himself from view behind a tall statue and peered at the figure, unsure if this person was friend or foe. From what he could tell, the person was small in stature, seemingly about Gabriel's height, and the clothing he wore seemed to be of an aristocratic nature. Just then, a voice cut through the darkness.

"Are you truly going to deny me a meal just because it's too early in the morning, you stupid fat old woman?" came a familiar voice, and Gabriel's grumbling stomach sank even lower.

"Ayden," he muttered to himself, making sure not to be heard.

The voice that came after was also familiar, but not as worrisome. "I told you once, young prince, and I will tell you again, you will wait until everyone else is awake before you can get breakfast! It's the rules! It's how things work here, *Your Grace*," Mrs. Fletcher said harshly to the snide youth, which made Ayden grumble in discontent. With clenched fists, Gabriel's cousin turned on his heel and stormed down the hallway, back toward the entrance hall.

Luckily for Gabriel, Ayden hadn't been paying much attention to what was around him, and once the fuming teen was out of sight, the young king slipped out of his hiding place and turned toward the kitchen. Stepping to the stone archway, he glanced inside the brightly lit room to see Mrs. Fletcher shaking her head angrily, her ginger locks cascading over her face. Gabriel could see that she was distraught, but the smells from the kitchen made his hunger grow rapidly. He cleared his throat roughly, making the stout cook jump in surprise as she turned to him. "Oh dear Lord! Your Majesty, you scared me, you did!" she exclaimed through a ragged breath.

Gabriel fully entered the kitchen. "My apologies, Mrs. Fletcher," he replied, resting his hand against the warm stones of the doorway. "I didn't mean to frighten you. It's just that I saw Ayden leaving few seconds ago, and I was wondering... was he trying to get breakfast?"

The red-haired cook shook her head one more time and looked down the corridor in the direction Ayden had gone, her expression angry and upset. "Aye, that snooty young whippersnapper was trying to get the fresh-est, best meal before everyone else," she shot back huffily, "and no one gets that meal except for the king!"

Gabriel put his hand on his audibly rumbling abdomen and looked at her with a smile. "The king, huh? Would I qualify for that meal, do you think?"

The short Scottish lady simply looked at him in confusion for a minute, then suddenly burst out laughing, making the other kitchen workers turn and stare at her before just as quickly returning to work. Mrs. Fletcher then sighed and wiped a small tear from her eye. "Oh my, Your Majesty, of course you do!" she responded happily, turning and beckoning him into the kitchen. "Come on, then. Let's get some food into you, Sire."

Gabriel smiled and followed the shout lady into the warm room, knowing that since Mrs. Fletcher was fond of him, he could get away with a lot more than anyone else could. It was good to be the almost-king! Gabriel was immediately met with the full, delicious aroma of what he had previously smelled. He looked to the right, and saw a few of the kitchen workers and other servants eating their breakfasts, small as they were. Upon seeing their future king, they stood and nodded respectfully or smiled to him and waved happily, to which he smiled and waved back. Then, he sat himself down at a free table near the rear of the room, and watched as Mrs. Fletcher placed a rather large plate of food in front of him consisting of scrambled eggs, two pieces of toast, two sizzling pieces of bacon, and two piping hot sausage links. He thanked her profusely and dug in. She smiled in return and walked back to the stoves to continue with her work, while Gabriel ate hungrily, his stomach no longer yelling at him.

Hurriedly, he finished his meal and took his dishes to the sink, then thanked all the kitchen staff and left the kitchen, his hunger satiated for the time being. By this time, most everyone had woken up and breakfast was beginning to be served. Soon the trial would begin, so Gabriel decided to take a detour into the ballroom for a minute. There, he sat on the stage that looked out over the entire room, and watched the band practice for a while. He thought about what would happen at the match today, hoping he didn't have to fight the one person he hated the most. But knowing Whittenburg, Ayden would surely be there.

He sat for a long while, pondering as per usual, then raised himself and left the ballroom, heading toward the entrance hall. However, as he neared the front of the castle, he noticed that a rather large crowd had gathered outside the throne room. Curious, he walked up to someone and was about to tap on their shoulder when he felt a hand grasp his collar, quite roughly, and pull him backwards away from the crowd. He tried to turn around to see who was dragging him, but their face was in shadow. "Hey! What's the big idea?" he protested.

"Shh!" came a hushed voice. It was a familiar voice, so Gabriel didn't struggle much more as they moved down the small hallway toward the king's entrance to the throne room. Soon, they reached their destination, and the hand that held his collar let go, allowing Gabriel to turn and face the person. He was shocked to find none other than Arthur, who was grinning widely.

"What was that about?" Gabriel asked in a harsh but hushed tone.

"Sorry about that, Sire, but we can't have you going in that way," he responded. "Caitlin and Whittenburg have been looking for you too."

Gabriel gave him a puzzled look. "Why?"

"Because your next trial starts right now."

"What! "

Wide-eyed, Gabriel stared at Arthur; he'd thought he had a few hours yet, so this unexpected turn of events shocked him... but then, perhaps he should just learn to expect the unexpected. Just then, he heard soft footsteps coming to a stop behind him. As he turned, he came face-to-face with Caitlin and his adviser, who were both looking amused.

"Ah, there you are, Your Highness," Whittenburg said.

"We've been looking everywhere for you," Caitlin chimed in.

Gabriel only looked at the two of them with his mouth agape. "Wha.... This is so sudden... I didn't expect the trial to be this early... I'm not prepared at all!"

"That's quite all right, Sire," Whittenburg responded. "That is what your friends are here for." He raised a hand and pointed to a small bench that mirrored the velvet curtain on the wall. On it rested his gleaming golden armor. "We have everything you need right here." Seemingly satisfied with the situation, the elderly scholar walked through the throne room doorway. Gabriel bit his bottom lip anxiously and looked down at the ground as Caitlin walked up to him and put her arm around his shoulders.

"Come on, Gabe, let's get you ready."

Gabriel sighed heavily and nodded to her, then walked to the bench with his armor laid out perfectly on it. Slowly and carefully, his friends began to slide the armor in place over his torso, shoulders, and legs, tightening the fastenings to fit it snugly. Gabriel often expressed how much he disliked being helped and how independent he was, but this time he allowed his friends to assist him without protest—just this once. The armor clinked and clattered and shifted uncomfortably, as always. Once everything was fitted to him as well as could be expected, he turned to his comrades. Both of them gave him a thumbs-up and beamed broadly.

"Looking good, best buddy," Arthur commented.

"You'll do great, Gabe," Caitlin agreed.

"Thanks, guys," Gabriel replied to his optimistic friends, "I don't think I could do this without you."

"Oh, sure you can."

"Now get out there and show them all what King Gabriel is made of!"

Gabriel let out a hearty laugh; then, without further ado, he turned to the violet cloth behind him and pushed through it.

As he entered the throne room, a loud eruption of applause arose around him. Peering about, he could see that the crowd inside the room was a lot larger than it had been the first time. He could also see that the benches that normally sat in front of the small raised stage were pushed back against the walls, making the tapestries behind them bunch up at the bottom a little. The thrones had been pushed back against the wall slightly as well, and a large mat had been placed out in the middle of the room. It looked more like a practice field than a place for royal endeavors. Smiling uncertainly at the excited audience, he made his way toward the middle of the room, where Whittenburg was standing and looking about. Upon seeing his charge, the old scholar grinned widely.

"Ah, there you are, Sire," he stated. "I was beginning to worry that you had gotten cold feet."

Gabriel shook his head casually. "You can't get rid of me that easily, David."

"It's good to see that you still have a sense of humor, Sire. That is most excellent in a king. Now: here comes your first opponent."

Gabriel peered through the grand wooden doors as the throng of people parted slightly, allowing a dark-haired, dark-eyed woman to walk in. Her hands were weathered and worn, as though she'd been working with them for many years. However, her face was kind. Strands of gray could be seen in her tied-back, jet-black hair, and her hazel eyes were aglow with fiery passion. On her torso she wore a dull iron breastplate, and on her forearms were thick iron gauntlets, all perfectly fitted to her.

She also wore a heavy pair of iron boots, though they were hidden under her long maroon dress. Gabriel knew who she was, and beamed as she neared them. "Hello, Lady Redwall," he said to her.

As the blacksmith came to a stop before him, she curtsied low and nodded. It was an oddity to have a woman blacksmith, Gabriel knew, but needs must; there had been no males in her generation of Redwalls, and hers was the greatest family of smiths in the kingdom. "Good day, Sire," she said in a rich contralto. "It is a great honor to be your opponent."

Whittenburg smiled and announced, "Miss Redwall, please bring forth the weapons." With another nod, the lady blacksmith walked toward the edge of the room, where a small arsenal had been set up along the wall: Gabriel recognized swords, maces, spears, staves, daggers, lances, morning stars, bows and arrows, and much more. Redwall gathered up as many of these as she could, and brought them over to the young king, who merely gave her and Whittenburg a look of confusion.

"What are these for?" he demanded, his mouth dry.

"This is to give you a chance to prove yourself with the weapon with which you are most comfortable, Sire," the elderly man replied flatly.

"I have almost no training at all in most of these!" he protested.

"Nonetheless, Sire."

Gabriel turned back to each of the weapons carefully. *So, the first test is my choice*, he mused, closely examining each item before him. He would have to choose something he knew he could win with, and finally, smiling to himself, he picked up the longbow, slinging the quiver of arrows over his shoulder with no difficulty. The various swords were tempting, but he was a crack shot with the English longbow.

Whittenburg nodded his approval. "Good choice, Sire," he said; then with another nod, the rest of the weapons were taken back to the wall from which they had come, leaving the blacksmith with a bow for herself. Just as the weapons made it back to their proper places, two more servants brought out thick, heavy targets made of bundled straw. On the targets were three colored circles: black on the outermost circle, then yellow, then red for the middle. Gabriel knew that he had to hit the middle for each shot, and was determined not to lose.

Whittenburg stepped in between the two of them to explain the rules. "Our first match is an archery tournament. Each competitor will have a total of five shots. Whoever has the most points at the end of the round wins. The points are as follows: the black circle equals five points, the yellow equals ten, and the red center equals twenty. Good luck to you both! You may now begin!"

Immediately, each competitor drew an arrow from their quiver and notched it to the bowstring. Slowly and carefully, Gabriel raised the bow so that it was level with his line of sight. He closed his left eye and focused on his objective, raising the bow just a bit to get the arc he needed, and then... SPANG!... THOCK! The arrow flew from the wooden bow and hit the target squarely. Applause arose once again from the crowd, but Gabriel paid no attention to it. He knew that if he were to give in to the pressure of pleasing the fans, he would lose the match for sure. Soon he heard the same low noise, as Mrs. Redwall's arrow hit the target as well. Hurriedly she drew another arrow to prepare for the next shot, and Gabriel followed suit. Again, the arrows flew and hit their marks, and another, and another.

Finally, the last shot was fired, and Whittenburg held up his arms to signal the end of the match. The audience fell quiet as they watched the elderly man walk up to the tall straw-woven structures, counting the points and pulling the arrows out roughly. With a smile, he walked back to the two opponents and leaned in so that only the two of them could hear. "I thank you both; this was a very close match." He then stood up and addressed the audience, "We have ourselves a winner, ladies and gentlemen! The scores were a mere five points apart, but with a score of 90 points, I am pleased to announce that the winner is... King Gabriel." The assembly of onlookers cheered once again, and Gabriel himself beamed in delight. Redwall walked to him and curtsied slightly, holding out her hand to him.

"Very well played, Your Majesty. I had no idea you were so skilled in archery."

Gabriel grinned and shook her hand. "It's one of my favorite sports, milady. Thank you, Miss Redwall." The ebony-haired blacksmith then bowed and left the room, trailed by servants hauling away the now-battered straw targets.

Whittenburg stood beside Gabriel, rustling some papers in his hands. "That was quite impressive, Sire," he said, peering at Gabriel over his spectacles. "Who knew you had such an affinity for the bow? However, the next match won't be as easy for you."

"I've noticed that it never is with you, David," the young man retorted. Whittenburg's smile broadened, and the two turned their attention back to the main entrance, to see who would walk through next.

To Gabriel's surprise, the next person to enter the makeshift sparring field was the knight captain himself, Sir Kameran. He was dressed in half his usual armor, wearing only a breastplate, greaves, and gauntlets. In his hand, he held a long wooden rod that looked heavy—and painful should it hit someone. He strode to the two of them with much confidence, a small smile playing upon his lips. As he arrived before his king, Sir Kameran knelt on one knee and bowed his head, resting the long weapon beside him.

"It is an honor to spar with you today, Your Highness," he said with due respect, then rose from the ground. Gabriel nodded firmly to him in response. Then, one of the servants brought to him a stave just like the one Kameran had brought, and he could only assume what his next match was going to be. Whittenburg, however, faced the audience and proceeded to explain the rules.

"For this match, both competitors will face off wielding a quarterstaff. The first to knock his opponent to the ground will be the winner." He then turned to Sir Kameran and Gabriel and spoke to them. "Fight fairly, gentlemen, and good luck to you both." Then he backed away and a loud clap sounded, signaling the beginning of the match.

At first, neither of then moved, unsure of who should cast the first strike. Then, Gabriel leaped forward and swung his staff at Kameran's chest, though he knew that making the first move would leave him open for a full-blown attack. The lanky soldier just shook his head and stepped to the side with ease, evading the attack, swinging his own weapon at Gabriel's unprotected backside. Quickly, Gabriel regained his footing and locked weapons with Kameran, the sound of wood upon wood echoing about the makeshift battlefield. The two pushed away from each other roughly and took a few steps back to analyze their situations. Gabriel could tell this fight wasn't going to be easy, especially since he was going up against the captain of the guard. How could he win this? He took a deep breath to calm himself, then launched himself again at Kameran, who blocked his attack with the staff.

The fight continued for a good ten or fifteen minutes, with neither side giving in. Gabriel was beginning to tire, panting slightly as he dodged and blocked Kameran's blows. Kameran was also becoming weary, each attack and block weaker than the next. Soon, the two were merely locked in a deadlock, and that's when Gabriel noticed how unsure Kameran's footing was. With a small smirk, he pushed the knight back hard and swung a leg at Kameran's feet. The soldier stepped back unsteadily to avoid the sweeping motion, but Gabriel was ready with another attack, and swept his staff toward Kameran's chest, connecting with a loud clang. Kameran let out an exasperated grunt and fell to his rear, holding his chest and wincing.

The audience then erupted in a sea of cheers as the audience rose from their seats, and Whittenburg lifted Gabriel's arm in the air in victory. He blinked a few times and peered about at the crowd, their happy faces making him smile slightly. The second part of the trial was over, and he had excelled! He felt proud of himself for this. Whittenburg lowered his arm and turned to him with a wide grin, as Kameran caught his breath and rose slowly to his feet. Gabriel held out a hand to help him up, which the tired soldier took gratefully.

"That was some blow, Sire," Kameran stated through ragged breaths, rubbing the spot on his chest where he'd been hit, "Where did you learn to fight like that?"

"I learned from the best," Gabriel said with a smirk, making the knight captain chuckle slightly.

"I guess Reginald taught you well, then."

"And you said you couldn't fight, Sire," Whittenburg tutted beside him, making Gabriel turn to the old man. "It seems as though you don't know your own strength, Your Majesty." Gabriel just smiled and nodded. Then Kameran was escorted out of the throne room by a servant, and the weapons were taken back to their shelves. Gabriel looked about and noticed that some of the townsfolk were exiting as well, and he turned back to Whittenburg.

"Where is everyone going, David?"

"We're going to give you a short break for now, so you can rest and recharge for your last match," he said, and as he turned away, his expression darkened slightly. "You'll need it, I'm afraid." Gabriel cast him a confused glance as he said this, but he decided not to think too much of it as Whittenburg walked away.

CHAPTER 12

GET TO THE POINT
(PART 2)

Gabriel sat down on the stone steps of the dais, looking out into the room, deep in thought. He was still wondering who the next opponent would be. At this point, he had a couple of people in mind, but knew that if he spent too much time thinking about it, he would only stress himself out. *I don't need to wind myself up right before the next match. It'll just end badly for me.* Sighing heavily, he ran a gloved hand through his sweaty hair and rose from his seat, turning toward the king's entrance. Before he exited, however, he noticed that one of the members of the Elder Council, a man by the name of William Hamilton, was speaking with his adviser about something. Curiously he peered at the two. *What are they talking about?* he wondered. Shaking his head, he figured it wasn't very important, so he made his way out of the throne room.

Once out in the hallway, he looked around to see if he could spy Caitlin and Arthur. Not seeing his companions, he strolled down toward the bench where his armor had been prepared for him. Carefully he slipped out of it and laid each piece on the bench where it had been, then he sat himself down and looked up. Above him was a grand portrait of the late king, his brother. It had been done when Reginald had first become king, so he was very young... though not as young as Gabriel was now. He wore the crown atop his head, a bit rakishly Gabriel thought, and a regal red cape across his shoulders.

"I miss you, Reggie," Gabriel whispered. He stared at the painting for a few more moments, his mind beginning to wander. He pondered whether his brother would be proud of him, and of how far he had come. *If only he could see me now*, he thought. His heart sank at the thought of never seeing this man again. His fists clenched slightly, and he hung his head. Reginald had taught him everything, or had tried to. Gabriel and Reginald had enjoyed spending time together, whether out for a stroll among the people, or playing games in the castle courtyard. The two were very close, even more so after the death of their parents, whom Gabriel didn't remember nearly as well as his brother. Reginald had been the only one he could turn to with his problems, his hopes, and his fears. Depression threatened to make roost in his heart as he let his mind linger on the memories that would never become reality again. Soon, however, his thoughts were interrupted by a maid, who had come to fetch him for his final match.

"Sire, they are waiting for you in the throne room," she said daintily, curtsying politely. Gabriel snapped out of his funk with a shake of his head and turned to her with a gentle smile.

"Thank you."

"Are you well, Sire?" she asked with a look of concern, offering him a glass of water that she had brought with her. Gabriel took the glass and quickly drained it, then returned it to her and nodded once again.

"I am now, Alyssa. Thank you," he repeated. Then he slipped back into his heavy armor, with a little difficulty, and followed the young lady back the way he had come.

As he pushed the velvet curtain aside and reentered the room, he could see that the crowd had gathered once again and were all anticipating his arrival. Upon seeing him, they clapped and cheered, making him smile. Then he turned to see who was also waiting for him, and his stomach churned in disgust and annoyance. The young man standing in the middle of the makeshift battlefield had brown hair and brown eyes, had donned silver armor, and carried a very sharp, deadly-looking iron blade. Gabriel walked to the center of the room, and as he faced the youth, an evil smirk spread across the other young man's face. "Ah, there you are, Cousin."

"Ayden."

"Are you ready to lose?"

"In your dreams."

"Now, gentleman," Whittenburg began as he walked up to the two of them, placing a hand on each of their shoulders, "this is going to be a clean fight. I don't want to see any dirty tricks like last time. Do you understand?" Both young men nodded, but Gabriel could already tell that his cousin wasn't planning on abiding by the rules. The malicious intent was evident in his eyes, and in his smile.

A servant then brought Gabriel his own blade, an iron sword just like Ayden's, then the two raised their weapons into position. Gabriel gripped the hilt with both hands. After this fight, he would be king at last, in more than name. The loud bang of a wooden rod echoed through the room, and Ayden immediately sprung forward with his sword raised. Gabriel easily blocked the attack with his own weapon, the clash of the swords reverberating off the stony walls around them. The power behind Ayden's blow was immense, though nothing Gabriel couldn't handle, and the wild look in his eyes was malevolent. The young king could tell that his cousin wasn't going to play fair; he figured Ayden would stop at nothing to dethrone him. Gabriel narrowed his eyes and gave his erstwhile relative a hard shove with his foot, making Ayden back away a little.

They faced each other once again with arms at the ready. Neither was going to make it easier for the other to win this battle.

Once more the boys launched themselves at each other, slashing and slicing with as much strength and finesse as possible. Ayden had a slight upper hand, since Gabriel was already tired from his previous contest, but the determined teen wasn't about to lose the throne to his conceited relative. Blow after blow, the boys struck, blocked, and dodged each others' attacks, neither giving the other an opening. Gabriel thought as he fought, *This is so much harder than anything I have ever encountered before...*

The sound of their swords clashing together repeatedly echoed around the room, making some of the audience cover their ears and cringe slightly. Others watched with wide eyes, jaws agape in admiration. A new crowd had gathered just outside the throne room, peering at the spectacle from the corridor. Guests and servants alike stopped to take in the fight and lend their support to their future king. Gabriel could feel all their eyes upon him as he swung the sword up with one hand to parry another attack. Sweat poured from his body, and he'd begun to start breathing hard as well. Ayden was a good swordsman, he had to admit; but Gabriel was determined not to lose his rights to the kingship, and continued to fight with all his strength.

The match continued for a good half an hour. Some of the spectators had left by then, to go back to work or otherwise. By this time, both Ayden and Gabriel were tired, sore, sweating, and almost out of steam. They stood with weapons locked, perspiration dripping from their faces as they panted hard.

"You... You won't win, Ayden," Gabriel stated through hard breaths.

"Oh no, Gabriel..." came Ayden's ragged reply, "It is you... who will not win. I... Won't... Allow it!" He pushed Gabriel back hard, causing him to stagger a little. Ayden saw his chance and swung his leg down at Gabriel's ankles to trip him, but Gabriel regained his balance in the nick of time and danced backward. He then backed away a little and raised his weapon defensively. Furious, Ayden jumped at Gabriel with sword raised. The young king saw this and stepped to the side, watching as his sneaky cousin overbalanced and fell to his knees. Gabriel saw this as an opening and kicked Ayden as hard as he could in the back, just as he had with Kameran. However, unlike Kameran, Ayden didn't fall so easily. In fact, the kick didn't seem to faze him at all. The other youth stood up slowly and turned to Gabriel. His eyes flashed with lunacy, and his teeth were bared as something like a growl emanated from him.

Gabriel's own eyes widened in astonishment, and he readied himself for another round. Ayden rushed toward him belligerently, slashing rapidly and wildly. Gabriel tried his hardest to block each blow as it came, but Ayden's speed was incredible.

Gabriel's foot slipped, and he slid backward a little, giving Ayden a small window of opportunity. He took another slice at Gabriel, and the tip of his sword connected with Gabriel's forehead, causing him to reel back and cry out in pain. Everyone in the room gasped loudly or shrieked in horror. Ayden backed away to revel in his achievement, and Gabriel held the cut on his head. The flesh was cut deeply, and hot blood trickled down toward his right eye, making it hard to see. His teeth clenched hard. He'd never felt agony like this before. He might be hardheaded, and the cut may not have been very deep, but it hurt worse than anything he'd ever felt.

Lord Whittenburg immediately rushed forward. "Your Highness!" he cried out, but before he could get much further, Gabriel held his free arm up to stop him.

"No," he said roughly, which made the elder man stop in his tracks, "Stay back, David. I'll handle this." Whittenburg stared at the young man in horrific astonishment, but he must have noticed the determined look in his liege's good eye. He nodded slowly, and backed up into the audience. Gabriel finally released his wound, so everyone could now see it. The bleeding had slowed; the blood seeped slowly down his brow and into his eye, as well as down his cheek. Ayden cackled as he held the bloodstained sword.

"What are you going to do, Gabriel?" he howled. "You can't even see properly. Just give up! You are not fit to be king!"

"Shut your damn mouth, Ayden," Gabriel seethed, standing tall and gripping the sword in both hands. "I'm sick and tired of listening to you and your power-hungry ideals. I'm tired of dealing with you. Maybe I'm not the best person to take my brother's place, and I may not know what I'm doing half of the time, but you're less fit to rule this land than a rabid wolf. Halcyon Ridge needs a good leader and a kind king, not a snot-nosed brat who has everything handed to him, who only cares about what he wants and nothing and nobody else. You already have entitlement to your own kingdom. Why do you want mine so bad?"

Ayden sneered, "I'll tell you why I want your pathetic excuse of a country—because my father won't give me my own! He's leaving it to my adopted brother, Seth, who my father believes is a better heir than I am!" His smirk turned to a grimace that widened as he faced Gabriel, "So if I get rid of *you*, and there is no one else of your bloodline to take the throne, then they HAVE to give it to me! I'll rule this land with an iron fist, and you'll be dead, so there won't be anyone to get in my way!"

Gabriel glared in rage at Ayden and gripped the sword's hilt tighter. "Laugh all you want, but I won't let you take the only thing I have left of my brother from me, Ayden!" he proclaimed as he raised the sword into position once again, then continued in a lower voice, "You'll have to pry this country from my cold, dead fingers."

"That can be arranged," Ayden said maliciously, bringing his bloody blade to bear, "I play for keeps, even if that means killing anyone who gets in my way!" He cackled wickedly and grinned at Gabriel, who only returned a hard look. He wasn't planning on dying today.

"I'd like to see you try!" he shouted. Ayden cackled once more, then lunged at his cousin. This time, Gabriel was ready, and stepped back, letting Ayden's sword come down in front of him. The wicked prince raised the blade quickly toward Gabriel's face again, but Gabriel blocked it in time, and the two were in a deadlock once more. Gabriel was struggling to keep his composure; his head hurt from the cut, he could barely see through his right eye, and he was worn out from the previous matches. He peered at Ayden, and noticed how he was focused totally on Gabriel's face. He wondered if his sly cousin would be too focused... and if he could break his concentration with a little distraction. Gabriel smirked slightly. It was a childish trick, but at the same time, he was dealing with a childish young man. "Hey, Ayden," he croaked.

"What?" the young man demanded.

"Your shoe's untied."

At that moment, Ayden gave Gabriel a genuinely confused look, as though someone had given him an extremely hard riddle to solve. Then, just as Gabriel had hoped, he looked down to see if what Gabriel had said was true. He was, in fact, wearing slippers. The teenage king saw his chance and grinned again, pushing Ayden back as hard as he could. Ayden fell backward onto his rear, his blade slipping from his hands and sliding over toward the stage on which the thrones sat. Ayden watched as his only line of defense flew away from him, a look of fear and shock in his eyes. Then, as he turned back to his cousin, he came face-to-face with Gabriel's blade, less than an inch from his nose. As Gabriel lowered the point and pressed it gently against his throat, a look of terror overtook Ayden's features as he stared up at his opponent.

No one moved; no one spoke. Though Gabriel had won the match, the situation was very tense indeed. No one knew what the young king would do. Would he execute Ayden on the spot, or just lock him up and throw away the key? Gabriel himself was having a hard time deciding. It was difficult to come to a reasonable solution, but the fact was, he had proven his point; he had shown Ayden that he was the stronger man, and what he could do should the need arise.

Gabriel closed his eyes for a moment, and let out a long breath. He wasn't heartless enough to kill a member of his family. Instead, he handed the sword off to a servant who stood nearby and held out an arm to his fallen foe. Ayden simply looked at him, dumbfounded. "What... What is the meaning of this?" he asked stupidly, taking his cousin's hand and rising to his feet.

"I'm not wicked like you are," Gabriel stated sternly, still glaring at him. "*That* is the meaning of this. I'll let you go this time, Ayden."

Ayden nodded quickly and anxiously, then began to walk away. As he passed Gabriel, the young king grabbed his cousin's arm roughly and held him for a minute, causing Ayden to jump and stare at him. Gabriel said in a low voice, "Don't think I won't remember what happened here. The next time you threaten my kingdom, it will be your last." Ayden's eyes widened a little further, and then Gabriel released him. The skittish youth took off past the audience, leaving Gabriel alone in the middle of the room.

Then, suddenly, as if glass had been shattered, an eruption of clapping and cheering arose, and the crowd began to close in around him. He looked up and around, a little dumbstruck after his victory. He had defeated his cousin fair and square, and for a moment he had forgotten where he was and what was going on. The audience began to chant his name, and Whittenburg appeared by his side, smiling wide.

"Congratulations, Your Majesty!" he exclaimed above the roar of the throng, "You have passed your last trial, and you surely put Prince Ayden in his place!"

Just then, Caitlin and Arthur grabbed Gabriel by the arms and hugged him tightly. "You did it, Gabe!" Caitlin cried out in excitement.

"Way to go!" Arthur agreed loudly. "We knew you could do it!"

Gabriel stared at his friends and his fans for a moment, allowing the glow of his win to come back to him, and beamed broadly. "Thanks, everyone," he responded proudly, hugging his comrades in return, "I couldn't have gotten this far without any of you."

"Aww, you could have done it anyway," his yellow-haired friend claimed. Arthur just nodded his head in agreement. "But you sure showed Ayden who was the real king!"

"Yeah," Gabriel said, "I guess I did."

"However, Sire," commented Whittenburg, "We need to get you to the surgeon to get your wound tended." Gabriel turned to peer at his adviser, then raised his hand to the cut on his forehead. The bleeding had stopped, but it still hurt, throbbing as the adrenaline in his body subsided.

"I agree," Arthur responded, "I'll take you there, Gabe. Or should I say, Your Majesty, King Gabriel the Merciful?" He swept into a bow, inviting Gabriel to walk ahead of him to the surgeon's chamber. The young king rolled his eyes, nodded, and allowed himself to be led away from the throne room toward the king's entrance.

Once the two had passed through the velvet curtain, the noise and cheering behind them quieted slightly. The two teens listened as Whittenburg directed everyone out of the throne room and announced that a feast would take place later that evening in the dining hall. Not wanting to be seen, Arthur led Gabriel down the back hallway and, making sure the coast was clear, crept down the other end of the hall toward the kitchens. The smells of cured meats and sweet food filled their nostrils, and it was hard for them not to stop and take a few things with them. Though they wanted a treat, they both knew that Gabriel's injury was more important than food, and they continued.

Soon, the boys came to the doorway that led to the back courtyard and the stadium. However, they didn't walk through the tall wooden doorway; beside the door were two sets of stairs. The one on the right led down into the dungeons, a dark and mysterious level where Gabriel had rarely set foot. The staircase on the left-hand side led to another tall tower, the tallest in the castle. This led to the lookout, where scouts would keep an eye out for enemies or intruders. They could see all the kingdom from up there. Gabriel hadn't noticed it before; he had been so focused on the trial at the outdoor arena that he hadn't been paying attention to his surroundings. He looked at his friend, who only pointed up the tall stairs to the left.

"The surgeon's office is up there."

"Lead the way."

Arthur cracked a small grin and nodded, taking them up the stony structure. This hallway was narrower than the one in Gabriel's bedroom tower, so they had to walk single file. As they ascended, the king put his hand on the cut yet again. It still stung like crazy... He would definitely have to be more careful in a sword fight. If this was how much a wound from a blade hurt, he could only imagine what pain he would feel if he were to lose a limb, or worse...

Soon they came to a door set into the stone about halfway up the stairs. The oaken door frame was covered by yet another velvet curtain, only this one was dark hunter-green in color. The boys looked at each other and nodded in certainty, then passed through the door together.

The interior of the room was bright, with lanterns hanging along the walls, supplementing the light filtering from the one window off to the left. A large blond man in a brown robe sat at a desk with a pen in one hand, adjusting his spectacles with the other. To the right of the desk, there lay a table with a medley of different medical tools; knives, bandages, catgut, gauze, rotgut alcohol that the surgeon claimed killed the tiny monsters that infested wounds, and many other awful-looking tools.

Arthur cleared his throat slightly, and the man whirled around quickly to peer at them. Upon seeing the king, he jumped to his feet and bowed hurriedly. "S-Sire!" he exclaimed, "Why, hello! What brings you to—" Before he could say more, Gabriel took his hand away from his forehead, revealing the gash. The doctor's hazel eyes widened a little, and he stood, striding quickly to Gabriel's side and examining the injury. "Sire, where did you get such a wound? It appears to be to the bone."

"Yes, and luckily I have a hard skull. Anyway... it's a long story, Sir Doctor Hamilton," the teen replied, to which the middle-aged surgeon simply gave him a wry look.

"Well, you can tell me all about it as I patch you up. Come, sit on the bench, please."

He ushered Gabriel toward the large wooden bench on the left side of the room, adjacent to the desk. The bench was wider than normal and looked specially made for someone to lie down. Gabriel sat upon the bench, and the doctor went to work, cleansing the wound with the rotgut, which stung worse than getting the wound had in the first place. He winced as he told his tale, and went a little pale as he saw the surgeon threat a length of catgut onto a hooked needle. "Bloody Ayden," the man muttered as he peered myopically at the thick thread. "I'm sorry. Sire, but the slash is bad because the blade was dull, and I do need to sew you up. It will hurt, unless you drink quite a lot of the alcohol and wait a bit. But it needs to be done, or the people will be calling you Gabriel the Scarred instead of Gabriel the Merciful. Unless you're the type who thinks scars look dashing...?"

Gabriel shook his head hurriedly, and rejected the whiskey bottle when it was offered. He suffered stoically through the seven stitches that followed, and hardly made any noise at all. Soon, the cut was clean and closed, and the surgeon was inspecting his work. Arthur, having watched his best friend being stitched up like a stuffed fowl, was a little green around the gills, but the wound had stopped bleeding and his king felt much better. Then the doctor began to bandage him up, winding a boiled and bleached linen strip around Gabriel's head. "Should heal up fine, Your Majesty," he said as he tucked in the bandage's edges. "Keeping it clean is very important now—I don't care what those quacks in London say. Come back daily so I can change the dressing, or I'll have to come looking for you, eh?"

"Thank you, Sir Dr. Hamilton," Gabriel said gratefully as he touched the bandage. The doctor merely smiled and nodded.

"All in a day's work," he replied, "Now, don't go getting into any more reckless sword fights, you hear?" As he said this, he waved a finger at the young noble.

"I won't."

"Good. Now, off you two go," Hamilton said, pushing the boys toward the exit. "You two need to get ready for the big feast tonight. Lots of pretty girls will be there!" The three chuckled as one, and then the two friends exited through the velvet curtain. With a goodbye wave to the good physician, they made their way down the narrow staircase once again, then took off to Gabriel's bedchamber. The procedure had only taken about fifteen minutes, but it had felt longer than that to Gabriel, for by now the sky outside had turned a deep shade of orange and red. He turned back from the window and sighed, rubbing his sore head.

"What a day, huh?" Arthur chirped from behind him.

"Yeah, what a day..."

"Come on, you don't want to be late for your own party, do you?" his comrade responded with a grin as he rummaged through his king's wardrobe. Gabriel just shook his head once again and laughed, before helping Arthur to pick out a suitable outfit.

CHAPTER 13

CONFESSIONS OF A TEENAGE KING

A little later that evening, Gabriel was sitting at the head of the long wooden table, speaking with Lord Whittenburg about his new duties and responsibilities. He was excited about his new role, but at the same time, he was also very nervous. He still had doubts about whether he would be a good fit for the throne, even though he had already obtained the rights to it and had proven both physically and mentally that he was ready to take the throne. He soon forgot this unease as he spotted his friends walking toward him. As they stopped before him, they bowed and curtsied respectfully to him.

"Greetings, King Gabriel, your Royal Highness," they said together with genuine respect. The king only grinned and nodded his head for them to stand.

"Arise, my friends," he responded as authoritatively as possible, causing all three of them to laugh.

"You really are ready for this, aren't you?" Caitlin said through her giggling. Arthur just beamed.

"I see you have become quite comfortable in that chair, Your Majesty," came a voice from above him. Gabriel leaned back to look for the source, and saw Sir Kameran hovering over him with a grin.

To his question, Gabriel smiled broadly. "I guess I have," he replied happily, then he turned to all four of them, "It's nice, you know, being here where my brother once was. I didn't expect to be thrown into the fire so quickly, but I suppose I came out on top. Now, I have the power to do what is right and what is fair, just like Reggie used to." Nostalgically, he looked up at the ceiling, as though he could see his brother's face in the wooden beams. "I hope I have made him proud."

"Oh, there is no doubt about that, Sire," Whittenburg said softly, causing Gabriel to turn to him. "I'm sure your parents and His Highness would be very proud of you indeed." He closed his eyes and nodded with certainty, while his friends followed suit, making Gabriel smile.

"Um.... E-Excuse me..."

Everyone in the room turned toward the voice, Gabriel smiling as he saw the young straw-haired stable girl, her fingers curled around the belt of her beautiful emerald-colored gown. The guests moved to the side a little to let her through, and Gabriel stared in awe. As Ashlyn slowly walked up to the table, a bright pink blush spread across her nose. Gabriel smiled warmly and stood up, walking to her and taking her hand in his own. "Ashlyn, thank you for coming," he said happily, "I'm glad you could make it."

The older men gave each other a confused look as Ashlyn chuckled sheepishly and pushed a lock of hair behind her ear. "W-Well, when one's presence is requested by the king himself, who could refuse?" she responded timidly.

This time, Whittenburg and Sir Kameran looked at Gabriel in puzzlement, but he had already thought of a plan. He had told Caitlin and Arthur ahead of time to distract the older men, so that he and Ashlyn could slip away quietly. At that moment, Gabriel winked at his friends, who took the hint and began to talk to the adults, allowing him and his special guest to sneak away from the party. They headed through the crowd and out into the entrance hall, where Gabriel led Ashlyn down the hall to the cherry-wood entrance to another room that he was very familiar with. Ushering her in, Gabriel looked around quickly to see if he had been followed, then walked into the ballroom behind her.

The inside of the ballroom was empty except for the band once again, who were practicing their Coronation Day songs and waltzes. They didn't seem to notice the two teens lurking about, slipping through a lead-paned French door that led out onto a balcony. The curtains had been pushed aside to let the light of the sunset and the rising moon creep in, making the room beyond glow. Once again, Gabriel looked about to see if anyone had trailed him, then he pushed the door closed and turned to Ashlyn. Her short hair had been tied up into a high ponytail with a green bow that matched her dress and her eyes. She stepped out onto the balcony above the courtyard and stood near the edge of the overhang, her hands gripping the railing as she stared into the beautiful sunset. Reds and oranges cast their warm glow across Halcyon Ridge, making it seem as though the kingdom were ablaze with light. Gabriel smiled at her enchanted expression and walked up beside her, placing his hand atop hers.

"It's beautiful, isn't it?" he asked, as he relaxed slightly and looked out at the town below. Ashlyn sighed contently.

"It sure is, Gabe..." she replied. Then, the blush returned to her cheeks. She pulled away from him shyly and turned her gaze toward the ground. "Um, so.... what did you want to talk to me about? Is it a secret?"

Gabriel took her hand from the rail and held it tightly, causing the young girl to blush even redder. "Ashlyn, there's something I've been meaning to tell you for a while now," he began, a little red flushing his face as well. "I know it may sound odd, but I have been feeling... quite strange, lately."

Completely oblivious to the underlying meaning, Ashlyn gasped in fright. "Oh no! Y-You're not hurt anywhere else, are you??" she exclaimed, feeling his head for any further injuries. Gabriel only laughed, and caught her worried hand in his own.

"No, no. It's not that at all. It's more..." He then took her hand and placed it on his chest, where his heart was beating, "...in here." Her face brightened even more as she stared up at him.

"W-what are you saying...?"

Gabriel smiled and sighed a little. "I don't know how to put this, Ash..." he began, looking directly into her deep green eyes, "but I've been thinking of you a lot. Ever since I first saw you, I've felt drawn to you. I wanted to help you so badly, but at the same time, I really wanted to get to know you better. So when Lord Whittenburg and I were able to free you from Ayden, I was happy to be able to talk to you more. I don't know why, but something inside me changed. I knew that you were the one..."

He looked down at Ashlyn, who had covered her mouth to stifle a gasp. Gabriel then took both of her hands and pulled her in close, so that their noses were almost touching. He could see her body trembling, though he didn't know if it was from excitement or fear. Smiling gently, he gazed into her eyes deeply once again. "I guess what I'm trying to say is..."

The king hesitated for a moment, not sure he had the courage to say what he wanted to say. *Oh come on,* he told himself, *you've shown more courage in the last month than you ever have; just buck up and spit it out.* Finally, he managed to say it: "...Ashlyn, I love you."

She gasped, and her cheeks flushed a dark crimson. She could only stare at him, speechless; and he knew exactly how she felt. Gabriel began to blush as well, giving her a gentle smile as he waited for her to say something. He knew that it was hard to say, and he only said it because he meant it. He had never loved another like he did Ashlyn, but the butterflies in his stomach fluttered as he waited. The anxiety of not knowing whether she felt the same was eating away at him slightly. A small breeze blew by them, lifting her hair up and away from her shoulders and cooling their burning cheeks. Finally, after what seemed like a long minute, Ashlyn began to speak slowly.

"I... I... I don't know what to say..."

"It's okay," Gabriel stopped her, a warm tightness twisting in his chest. "I'll understand if you don't feel the same way. I'm sorry I pulled you away from your duties for something so petty." He let go of her hands and bowed gallantly to her, then turned to walk back toward the French doors of the balcony.

"Wait!" she exclaimed, causing him to stop short and turn back to her in astonishment and confusion. She turned her face down quickly and twisted the edge of her dress once again, shyly as ever.

"What is it?" Gabriel asked her.

"I love you too, Gabriel," she whispered. "Though it's not proper for a commoner to love her king that way, I do."

His eyes widened to the size of saucers. Seeing his reaction, the girl took a deep breath and continued, "I knew it from the moment you saved me. I knew that I loved you when I no longer had to be told how to feel... Gabriel, that kiss we shared in the garden that night meant more to me than anything in this world. I don't know if we can ever be together, because of our social standings... I mean, you're a king! I'm just a stable hand..." She looked away one more time, even more nervous and sad than before.

Gabriel, on the other hand, beamed from ear to ear and nearly jumped for joy. The girl he had fallen in love with had reciprocated his feelings, making him one of the happiest men alive! His chest tightened more, as if his heart was about to burst with happiness. He walked up to her and threw his arms around her, hugging the young maiden tightly, which surprised her greatly. "I don't care where you come from or what your social standing is, Ash," he declared, "I'm just happy to have met my soul-mate!" Ashlyn stared up at him, her emerald eyes quivering slightly. The shock was evident on her face, but Gabriel could see excitement in her eyes as well, a small grin creeping upon her lips.

"Gabriel..." Her voice was soft as she spoke fondly, reaching up to caress his cheek.

"Ashlyn..." he murmured, his left hand moving to her waist to pull her in close. Slowly, carefully, Gabriel pressed his lips against hers in a soft, gentle kiss. Ashlyn closed her eyes and returned it, leaning into his embrace. They stood there, locked in each others' arms, for what seemed like eternity; to Gabriel, it felt like time had stopped altogether. Not even the wind interrupted them.

Finally, they pulled away from their kiss and looked at each other lovingly. It was a magical moment that he was sure they would both remember until the end of time. The fresh moonlight made their skin glow more than it already had, and the stars twinkled high in the velvet black sky above them. Gabriel held her close and stared into her eyes. "I never want to let this moment go."

"Me either. I wish it could be like this forever, Gabriel."

Gabriel sighed happily, but then his expression fell as he stepped away from her and held her at arm's length.

"But it can't. So before we go back to the chaos of the dining hall...." He held onto her hands and knelt on one knee, making Ashlyn gasp and cover her mouth excitedly.

"Oh Gabriel... Are you...?"

The young king smiled and nodded. "My dear, you mean the world to me," he started, still holding her hand, "I've been meaning to ask you this since the moment I realized that you were the only woman for me... Ashlyn Roseleigh, will you marry me? Will you be my queen?"

The lady blushed brilliantly maroon, but smiled widely. "Of course I will!" she exclaimed, wrapping her arms tightly around his neck. Gabriel grinned as well. He couldn't have been any happier. He had his kingship, he now had a queen to rule by his side, and he had the trust and loyalty of his friends and followers. He couldn't have asked for more.

The two of them spoke excitedly and animatedly as they made their way back to the dining hall, holding hands tightly the entire way. They were a bit worried that Lord Whittenburg would say that the marriage wouldn't be allowed because of their ages or very different social classes, but neither of them worried for long. Their love for one another would push through anything, or so Gabriel told himself. Soon, they returned to the dining hall, where they finally realized their hands were interlocked, releasing them before anyone noticed. They stood outside the door and looked at each other. "Will I see you tomorrow?" Gabriel asked his new fiancée.

"But of course, Your Highness," Ashlyn responded, curtsying to her future husband and king. The two exchanged a few chuckles, then embraced once more before Gabriel sent her on her way back home, returning to the dinner.

The next day, Gabriel woke in a lighthearted mood, stretching in an upward motion and swinging his legs off the bed. His toffee-colored hair was a mess, so he grabbed the nearest comb, a fine narwhal-ivory one that had belonged to his father, and began to straighten it out. As he placed the comb on the night table beside him and stood up, he half-expected to hear a knock on his door, but none came. He shrugged it off and got dressed. Once he was satisfied with how he looked, he exited his room and locked the door behind him. Then he peered around the cobblestone staircase, his jaw dropping in awe.

The tower, and all the castle, had been elaborately decorated overnight. No longer were the walls dreary and gray; they were now brightly arrayed with streamers, bunting, and tapestries—some of which, he was astonished to see, appeared to show him and his exploits... there was one where he was jousting, and was that one of his sword fight with Ayden? Wow, that was quick! New banners lined the stair rail, and a long red carpet had been laid out over the steps, embellished with gold trim and his family's coat-of-arms woven into the fabric. As he admired the new decor, servants rushed about, preparing sleeping quarters for all the guests. The village and royal stables had to make room for the coaches and horses that accompanied some of the guests as well. You would have thought that it was Gabriel's coronation day already, with how busy everyone was, but the actual coronation wouldn't take place until the next day.

Still, there was much to do, and as Gabriel tried to avoid the hustling workers, he had a plan of his own that he needed to fulfill before tomorrow. He would first find Ashlyn, as they had agreed, and then they would go to Whittenburg to make their case for their marriage. The king was more than determined to marry the girl that he loved, no matter what, and was ready to do anything it would take. He narrowly evaded a large coronation day cake as it came through the entrance hall door, then squeezed by the entering guests and staff and made his way toward the castle stables. The bustle increased as he walked the pale stone path. The servants rushed about preparing for the big day, and guests of all kinds loitered about the castle grounds, conversing with each other or taking in the sights. Along the way, Gabriel noticed a few people he had previously met, such as Duke Ericson and Duke Archibald, both of whom had been present during his summit meeting. He waved to the two as he passed, and continued on his way.

When he reached the stables, he briskly passed a few of the stable hands who were rapidly working to get the horses ready, walked straight to Ashlyn's door, and knocked on it twice. However, he heard no movement inside, nor did he hear her call out to him. Puzzled, he knocked on the door once again, but there was still no answer.

"Ash? Ashlyn? It's me, are you there?" he called, knocking once more. Out of politeness, he didn't try to open the door, but instead turned and put his hand on his chin, thoroughly confused. One of the stable workers saw him like this and stopped before him.

"Sire? Are you looking for Ashlyn?" the girl asked.

Gabriel looked up at her and nodded firmly. "Yes, I am," he stated. "Have you seen her this morning, Jocelyn?"

"No, Sire, I haven't," replied the girl. "As a matter of fact, I don't think she returned home last night."

"What? What do you mean?" Gabriel asked, his eyes widening in worry. "Is that normal for her?"

"No, not at all," the stable hand said, shaking her head, sending her black curls tumbling. "She usually comes home right after dinner, and stays there all night, unless she decides to visit with the horses for a bit. I don't know where she could be."

Gabriel felt a frisson of worry, and once again, his hand rose to his chin as he looked at the ground in thought. If Ashlyn wasn't home, where could she be? He thanked Jocelyn for the information, then he left the barn to go look for his bride-to-be.

Finding Ashlyn wasn't going to be easy. He didn't know all the places where she would go to ease her mind, other than Solstice's or her own horse's stalls, but he had to try. He checked the stalls, then the rest of the stables, but no luck. Well, she hadn't returned home last night, so she must have stayed the night with someone else. *Right?* he told himself, trying not to worry. His mind immediately turned to Caitlin; perhaps Ashlyn had spent the night with her new friend. With this thought in mind, he returned to the castle, pushing his way through the throng until he reached the tower to the summit room. Sir Kameran's bedchamber was up there, as well as Caitlin's. He trotted up the tall staircase toward her room, knocking on the door as he reached it. He was unsure of whether she would be there, but he had to check.

However, once again, there was no answer. Perhaps Caitlin wasn't there. Shrugging and sighing a little, he turned back and began to walk toward the kitchens.

Then an idea popped into his head. Maybe she had stayed with Mrs. Fletcher! He weaseled his way through the crowded corridor again, and continued down the hallway toward the kitchen. However, as soon as he arrived, he could see that the cooks and bakers were very busy indeed; grand meals were being prepared, and the aroma of cured meats, baked sweets, and other flavorful dishes filled the hallway around him. He smiled as he took in the smell, but he only did this for a minute before looking around to see if he could spot Caitlin or Ashlyn. Seeing neither one of them, he sighed heavily and left. He took the short cut through the back entrance and walked back around to the front of the castle, and kept on looking as he walked. *Where could she have gone?* he wondered.

He was running out of ideas when he suddenly thought of Madam Winter and Arthur; perhaps she had gone to stay with them. He sped through the middle of town toward the local inn, then took a side street that veered off to the right. The street ended at the beginning of a dirt road, and soon, Gabriel could see a small cottage with smoke billowing from the chimney. The stones of the house were old but strong, and the place was well kept. He could also see his best friend outside with an ax, hacking away at a large pile of wood. His shirt was drenched in sweat, his fiery locks matted to his head. As Gabriel neared, Arthur wiped the perspiration from his brow and looked up, spotting his regal comrade and waving. "Gabe! What brings you here?" he called.

"Hey, Arthur. Did Ashlyn spend the night with you guys?" the young king asked.

Arthur merely crossed his arms and gave Gabriel a stern look. "Now, you know Mum won't let me have any girls at the house," he said. "She wouldn't even let Caitlin stay overnight…" he seemed to catch himself.

"Caitlin? Why would Caitlin ever stay over at your place?" Gabriel demanded.

"Oh! Um, no reason," Arthur said, his face redder than his hair. "But no, Ashlyn isn't here. Why do you ask?"

Gabriel shrugged off his confusion about the Caitlin comment, though it sparked a suspicion in the back of his mind. He shoved it aside. "Ashlyn didn't return home last night, and I don't know where she is."

Arthur's eyes widened. "Do you think Ayden might be involved?" the redhead asked tentatively.

Gabriel stared at him, slightly bewildered. "Oh Lord, I hope not," he said slowly, as he turned to look at the inn where the Prince of Holheim was staying. "I have to go check it out."

"Now, hold on," Arthur said, putting the ax down. "I'll go with you. I'll just let Mum know where I'm going, right?" He rushed inside, while Gabriel waited at the end of the walkway. A few minutes later, the boys were making their way back toward the town square. It was mid-morning, so the streets were even busier than before, and they found it hard to find a place to walk at all. Because many of the people in the crowd were from out of town, they didn't recognize Gabriel, so they didn't automatically make way for him. Finally, they were able to jump in and follow the flow of traffic to the entrance of the Golden Goose Inn, where Gabriel knew his cousin was staying, and the two of them slipped inside.

The inn was just as crowded as the rest of town, but it seemed comforting inside, beautifully decorated as it was with dark-green painted walls and fine hardwood floors. A few potted flowering plants lined the edges of seats that were scattered about the front foyer, but the boys didn't have time to stop and admire these decorations. They pushed and shoved their way to the front desk, where the guests could check in or out and ask for room service, and looked up at the innkeeper, a short, scrawny lady who looked like she ate very little, with large puffy lips painted a dark crimson and very curly orange locks that were peppered with strands of white. The strange lady gave them a languid look and smiled coyly.

"Well hello, gentlemen!" she cooed, twirling her dry tangerine hair around her forefinger. "Might I help you with something today, Your Highness?"

"Lady Rosetta, I'm looking for someone," Gabriel stated. "An attractive young lady, my age. Her name is Ashlyn Rosenleigh. She's five foot two, has blonde hair, and bright green eyes. Have you seen her?"

In no hurry, Rosetta looked up at the ceiling thoughtfully and put a long-nailed hand upon her chin, stroking it gently and humming slightly in thought. Arthur turned away in disgust. Then the innkeeper snapped her fingers and looked back at him with a giant grin. "Why yes! I did see a young girl by that description!" the odd-looking woman exclaimed, loud enough for the whole foyer to hear, "She was with that godawful Prince Ayden! They left town early this morning, though they didn't say where they were going."

Arthur and Gabriel exchanged bewildered glances. "Oh no!" they said in unison, and without thanking the lady, they ran back out into the busy street. Once there, Gabriel turned to his friend with a look of determination. "Go find Caitlin and gather up some of the guards," he demanded. "And Sir Kameran, if you can," to which his friend only turned to him with an anxious expression.

"What are you going to do, Gabe?" Arthur asked, to which Gabriel only turned toward the town gate, glowering furiously.

"I'm going on a manhunt."

"No way!" Arthur exclaimed, shaking his head and frowning hard, "There's no way I'm letting you go by yourself!" Gabriel's glare turned back to him, and Arthur wilted as he saw the fire in his king's eyes. He said nothing more, just nodded and raced off toward the castle. Gabriel faced the town gate for a few moments, then he too sprinted at top speed toward the courtyard.

Before he reached the courtyard archway, he veered to the right and raced as fast as he could toward the castle stables. He didn't ask any of the staff for help as he hurriedly gathered his horse's equipment and threw it on Solstice. The stallion seemed to be worried as well, for he snorted and jerked his head anxiously as Gabriel attached his bridle. Then, once everything was ready and fit, the determined young man literally jumped onto the saddle and snapped the reins. Solstice dashed out of the stable, past the yelling stable hands, past the screaming and running people in the town square, and past the alarmed soldiers guarding the town gates. There was no stopping him; he and Solstice galloped on, determined to find Ashlyn.

"Don't worry, Ashlyn," Gabriel said aloud as they sped along the path just outside of the gates, "Just hold on until I get there." The horse whinnied once again and jerked its head toward a small opening in the forest, the very same one the four friends had visited a few days prior. Gabriel nodded and ushered Solstice toward the entrance, racing at top speed into the turn. "Just you wait, Ayden," the young king said. "I'm coming for you..."

CHAPTER 14

BLOOD TIES

The woods seemed darker and more mysterious than he remembered. As the two galloped along the path, no sound could be heard other than the pounding of Solstice's hooves on the packed dirt. Leaves and tree branches hung low enough to graze the young king's head, and they narrowly evaded a large tree root that thrust up out of the ground. Gabriel's mahogany hair fluttered atop his head, and his focused blue eyes stared at the path ahead, awaiting the sight of the lakeshore.

As soon as he judged they were near, Gabriel pulled the reins back and spoke softly to Solstice to slow the mighty animal, afraid that the loud thundering of his hooves would give them away. They soon caught sight of the lake, sunlight sparkling off its surface. Gabriel took a good look around; there didn't seem to be any good place for his devious cousin to be hiding. He looked at his steed. "Are you sure she's here, Solstice?" he asked.

As if to answer his question, the horse snorted softly and took the lead, walking the two of them toward the back of the lake, a place he hadn't investigated yet. Against the rock wall that Gabriel hadn't noticed before was the entrance to a cave that led deep into the basalt bedrock. Shocked at his horse's knowledge, he slid out of the saddle and stood beside Solstice, patting his neck gently. Then he walked Solstice to a nearby tree with a low branch and secured his reins loosely.

"When the others show up, let them know where to go, all right?" he told his steed, who sniffed loudly and nudged his handler. Gabriel smiled slightly and patted the tuft of hair between the magnificent beast's ears, then walked toward the mouth of the cave, entering it warily.

The dark, shadowy rock was damp, so Gabriel had to be careful where he put his hands. He tread carefully, so as not to make too much noise, for he was hoping to sneak up on Ayden and get the upper hand. However, the farther in he traveled, the darker the cave became, until he could barely see his own hand in front of him. His boots scuffed softly against the dirt, and he could feel occasionally sharp stones sticking out of the soil. If he were to fall, it would hurt. He knew that if someone were to creep up behind him and take him off guard, he wouldn't be able to stop them, at least not very well. *I have to be extremely careful,* he cautioned himself, continuing his trek.

Soon, he could see faint lantern light ahead of him, the flame's glow flickering along the dark rocks. Just then, he heard a faint sound; it sounded like a footstep just behind him, so he didn't dare move. He halted immediately, not making another sound. Was it just his imagination playing tricks on him, or had someone followed him into the cave? He was unsure, but his fists clenched as he readied himself for a fight.

He spun and swung at the source of the sound—but there was no one there. His boots clattered against the rocks below him, and his hand slipped along the wall, making a small squeaking noise as he skinned his knuckles. His heart skipped a beat; he knew he would be found now! For a few moments, he stood stock-still and waited, listening for any sign that he had been noticed. Not hearing anything, he turned back and was about to continue—when he came face-to-face with a red-haired woman in a purple robe, a wicked grin upon her face.

Startled by her sudden appearance, Gabriel tried to back away, but quickly stumbled and fell, a sharp stone stabbing his hand. Yelping in pain, he felt himself being pulled to his feet by a pair of dainty yet surprisingly strong hands. They held his arms firmly behind his back, long painted nails digging into his skin and causing him to wince slightly. "Hello, Your Royal Highness," the strange lady cooed maliciously. The voice was familiar, and Gabriel nearly growled as he tried to look at her.

"Isabelle... You're Ayden's personal attendant!" he said in a hushed, harsh tone. The woman holding him firmly merely snickered and gripped his arms tighter.

"So you DO remember me, Sire!" she replied, reaching up to his cheek and pinching hard. Gabriel shook her hand off him and scowled menacingly at her. Isabelle only grinned wickedly at his glare and pushed his arms forward, ushering him further into the cavern. "My master will be pleased to see you."

Gabriel hung his head in shame; he had no choice but to let her lead him. The only good part about being captured was that he could finally find out where Ashlyn was hidden, and maybe even rescue her.

They trudged on through the damp cave toward the source of the light, and as they did, Gabriel could hear two voices, both making his heart drop in worry and anger. At first the voices sounded like whispers, low and inaudible; but the closer they drew, the more the young king could hear of the conversation, and the more he didn't like what it was about.

"You tell me what I want to know, you stupid girl, or else..."

"No... No, Ayden, I won't tell you anything about..."

Ashlyn's green eyes widened as she turned and saw Isabelle and Gabriel enter the room, Gabriel's head still hanging low. He emitted a loud grunt as he was shoved to the dirt floor, causing Ayden to turn and stare. "Look who I found skulking about," the sultry woman gloated, pushing a lock of ginger hair behind her purple-clad shoulder. At first Ayden seemed astonished to see his cousin; however, a wide, wicked smirk spread across his face, and he walked to the boy on the ground, kneeling down to him and grasping him firmly by the hair before yanking his head upward. Gabriel let out another cry of pain, and looked up at Ayden with a nasty glare.

"Well, well, well," the malignant teen snickered, gripping Gabriel's mahogany locks tighter, "Look who showed up. Come to save your future queen, have you? How sweet." He shoved his cousin's face back into the dirt. Gabriel let out a grunt and raised himself onto his hands and knees, coughing to get the sand out of his lungs.

"Gabriel!" Ashlyn cried as she tried to run to his side.

Before she could take two more steps, however, she was caught and held firmly by Isabelle, whose menacing grin grew wider. "I don't think so, kitten," she said coyly. "The boys have some unfinished business to attend to."

Ayden laughed wickedly and walked to the farther side of the small cave as Gabriel rose to his feet. He continued to spit sand from his mouth as he turned his glare toward his cousin. "What does she mean, Ayden?" he demanded.

"What else could she mean, dearest cousin?" the wicked prince sneered, walking up to a boulder. On it lay two sharp, silver blades. Gabriel's eyes widened as he gazed anxiously upon them. *A duel? Another swordfight? What would Ayden hope to accomplish with another match?* However, as Ayden returned to his position with said swords in hand, Gabriel realized what his cousin was up to: he had lost to Gabriel in an official match, so he was going to have one here, where there was no one to set guidelines and rules—and no one to stop Ayden from trying to kill him this time. "Have you figured it out yet, cousin?" Ayden spat at him, tossing one of the swords at Gabriel's feet. Gabriel only scowled in determination and reached down for the sword, picking it up and positioning it in front of him. He wondered if it was booby-trapped, or flawed so that it would break during the duel. He wouldn't put anything past a blackguard who would kidnap the woman he loved.

"This won't accomplish anything," Gabriel said, "whoever wins."

"Oh, I won't lose this time, because I know your weakness," Ayden hissed, pointing his blade toward Ashlyn and Isabelle. Gabriel peered at them, and his eyes widened in fear at what he saw. Isabelle had a small iron dagger pressed lightly against the great vein in Ashlyn's throat.

"No!" cried Gabriel, lowering the sword and pointing to them,

"Ayden, this is low, even for you! Just let Ashlyn go; it's me you want."

"I don't think so. You fight me, or the girl gets her throat cut." Gabriel's eyes flickered between Ashlyn and Ayden, worry and unease eating away at his insides. He had to choose... Finally, with a heavy sigh and a glowering scowl, he brought the blade up once more. Isabelle would try to hurt Ashlyn if Ayden lost, but maybe he could be fast enough to disarm her after he beat Ayden.

That was all the time he had for thinking. Without further hesitation, Ayden launched himself into action, and it was do-or-die time.

Ayden was a skilled fighter, Gabriel had to give him that; but when he was wild and crazy, as he was now, he didn't pay attention to what he was doing, and made plenty of mistakes. That was the angle Gabriel would use to beat him. He would get Ayden to the point of pure madness, then take the prince by surprise and knock him on his rear, just like last time. However, Isabelle must have been able to read his movements, for she yelled out over the clashing of metal on metal, "Don't even think about it, King Gabriel. If you try anything funny..."

She didn't have to say anything more, as she pressed the blade of the dagger into the girl's neck. Though it was not enough to cut her deeply, Ashlyn still cried out painfully as a line of red appeared at the point of contact. A growl of frustration erupted from Gabriel's throat as he pressed the fight. However, no matter what he did, he could not overpower Ayden; and anytime he tried to fight dirty like his cousin, a yelp could be heard from the sidelines as the short blade threatened to plunge deeper into Ashlyn's skin. *Damnation,* he thought, *What am I going to do?*

Soon, both boys were tired and sore, and Gabriel hadn't gained any advantage whatsoever. Ayden was winning, if only because he was cheating and using Ashlyn against him. The young king wiped a bead of sweat from his brow. Where were Caitlin and Arthur? They should have been there by now! Normally, they would have already swooped in and saved the day; but this time, it looked like he'd have to save himself, and Ashlyn too.

At this point, he knew, the chances of either of them making it out of the situation alive were slim, at best.

As Ayden slashed at him once more, Gabriel clenched his teeth, and glared at his cousin behind locked blades; then, as he glanced over at Isabelle and Ashlyn, he got the faint inkling of a plan. Maybe he was fighting the wrong person... If he could get the red-haired lady away from Ashlyn, or at least get her to drop the knife somehow, then he could grab his fiancée and escape from the cave. With this thought in his head, he continued to block and dodge Ayden's attacks.

Slowly, Gabriel inched the battle closer to the ladies, hoping that Isabelle would be unaware of how close he had gotten to them. However, just as he was about to turn and reach for Ashlyn, Isabelle stepped away from him, pulling the girl with her. At that moment, Gabriel stepped back just in time to avoid Ayden's sword as it almost grazed his nose. He then backed away a little and stood his ground. Until now, he hadn't realized the strain that the battle had put on him; every muscle in his entire body ached horribly, and his chest began to sting with every strained, ragged breath. He panted hard, keeping his eyes on his opponent. *How much longer can I go on like this...?* he wondered.

Ayden, on the other hand, didn't look tired at all; in fact, he was flexing his muscles and stretching nonchalantly, as though the fight had done nothing to him or his physique—which enraged the young king even more. It took all of Gabriel's willpower just to get up the strength to move, every action he made restricted and slowed. At this rate, he would lose for sure, which only meant one thing: death. Ayden was not merciful at all, and he wanted his cousin's throne too badly to reconsider any type of compromise or negotiation.

Without another thought, Gabriel refocused himself and blocked another attack.

This went on for a while as the boys exchanged attacks, both blocking every one of them. Only once did Gabriel slip up, a mistake he really couldn't afford to make. His foot slipped as he attempted to block one of Ayden's downward slashes, and the blades missed each other. Ayden's sword cut deeply through the skin of Gabriel's arm, causing it to bleed freely and roar with pain. Gabriel cried out and backed away, grabbing the wound. Ashlyn cried out as well, and struggled mightily to get away, but the much larger Isabelle just held her tighter and pressed the small blade tighter to her throat. All the while, Ayden was chuckling evilly, walking toward his cousin with a most malicious grin.

"Hah! You are weaker than you appear," he crowed as he neared his target. "How does it feel to be humiliated in front of your beloved? I just wish your friends could be here to see you be slain by the hand of their new king."

Gabriel continued to put pressure on his wound, blood trailing down his arm slowly and steadily. The pain was intense... *So this is what it's like to be in a deadly duel*, he thought. *This isn't some courtly match with rules... I'm in a true life-or-death situation here. If I'm not more careful...*

He knew the outcome should he fail, which renewed his determination. Gabriel shook himself out of his funk and raised the sword painfully, to which Ayden only smirked malignantly and mirrored him. "Ready to hand over your kingdom yet, Gabriel?"

"Never. Not to you."

"Suit yourself, then," Ayden said as he shrugged lazily. His arrogant manner was enough to prod Gabriel into motion again. Anger and pure adrenaline made him forget just how much pain he was in, and he couldn't keep his composure any longer. Angrily, shouting, he lashed out at his cousin, who dodged the attack. Then, in one swift motion, Ayden brought the sword down and laid open the back of Gabriel's leg just as he attempted to move out of the way. Once again, Gabriel yelled in pain, this time falling to one knee. He wouldn't give up...

The pain fueled his rage more, driving his to his feet. He twirled around to strike, but Ayden quickly parried the blow, knocking Gabriel's sword back just enough so that he could kick Gabriel in the chest just below his breastbone. Unable to make a sound, unable to breathe, Gabriel fell backward onto his hind end, dropping the sword from nerveless fingers. Just as he caught his breath, he looked up to find the sharp end of a blade pointed directly at his nose. A look of pure terror crossed his face; this was the end for sure. His teeth clenched tightly as he glared at Ayden. He refused to yield, even though it was clear he had lost to the very person he despised so much.

Just then, there was a very faint sound. Though it was quiet, it echoed about the cavern, causing the four of them to look suddenly toward the source. Gabriel couldn't quite tell what it was, but it sounded as though a horse nearby had whinnied, and footsteps slowly approached them.

Ayden and Isabelle were so focused on the sound that they failed to pay attention to their victims. Gabriel took full advantage of the situation and quickly grabbed the blade next to him in both hands. He hadn't the strength to kill his cousin, but he did swing the blade as hard as he could and gave him a nasty gash in his side. Ayden shrieked like a schoolgirl as the blade pierced his skin, dropping his own blade and falling to the ground, clutching his side in agony. At the same time, Gabriel heard a loud, shrill yelp and turned just in time to see Isabelle release Ashlyn from her grasp and drop the dagger to the ground. She was holding her bleeding nose and wincing hard. Ashlyn landed in the dirt, rubbing her aching head for a minute, then scrambled to her feet and hurried to Gabriel's side.

Meanwhile, whoever was making the sounds continued to approach, the sound of hooves echoing against the wet rocks and walls. Soon, shadows began to dance along the rocky interior from a handheld lantern, and a voice emerged from the darkness. "Gabriel!"

The voice was very familiar; and no sooner had he thought this than the pair he had been looking forward to seeing rushed into the cavern. As they took in the scene, Caitlin and Arthur's expressions changed from worry to half-relieved, half-horrified. They weren't alone. Behind them strode Kameran, the knight captain himself, with a handful of guards. As Arthur and Caitlin ran to Gabriel, the soldiers converged on the other two, swords in hand.

When his friends threw their arms around him tightly, Gabriel cried out in pain and winced; but he was glad to see them. "We were so worried about you, Gabe!" Caitlin cried, as tears flowed from her bright blue eyes.

"Promise you'll never do something stupid like that again, all right?"

Arthur agreed sternly. Gabriel smiled as much as he could, and just nodded. As they let him go, Ashlyn, who had been curled up beside him in
a ball of tears and hurt, slowly wrapped her arms around his waist and
sobbed into Gabriel's blood-stained shirt.

"You idiot!" she screamed suddenly, causing everyone in the room to
look at her, astonished. "You could have been killed!" Gabriel just looked
down at her, bewildered by the statement. As she sobbed, he could feel
her hot tears against his burning skin. He had no idea what she must be
feeling, though, so he only put a gentle hand on her back and rubbed
softly.

"I'm sorry, guys, for worrying you..." he responded weakly, pulling
his future queen closer to him and looking down at her. "Especially you,
Ashlyn."

"Why did you do it?! Why did you come alone?!" the straw-haired girl
continued loudly, turning her tear-stained face up to look at him, "What
you did was idiotic and dangerous! You could have died, Gabriel! Tell
me why!"

Gabriel's eyes widened at her remarks. He knew that she was scared
and worried, but this demand was so unlike her. All he could do was smile
and hold her by the shoulders as he looked into her worried emerald eyes.
"Well, besides the fact that I *am* an idiot," he said, "I was so worried about
you, Ash."

She just stared at him, blushing furiously, as he continued, "I couldn't
find you. When I realized Ayden had you, I went after you that very moment. Ashlyn, I love you, and I don't ever want to lose you. You're too
important to me."

Ashlyn's eyes were wide as she stared up at him, completely astonished. Being told he loved her was one thing; but proving it this way drove
the lesson home. Taking advantage of her silence, Gabriel embraced the
trembling girl. All the fear and anxiety seemed to melt away from her
body as she leaned against him and relaxed into his arms.

Soon, more knights and other soldiers arrived to collect them. Ayden
and Isabelle were taken into custody, hauled away over Kameran's steed

with hands and feet bound so they couldn't escape. Isabelle scowled harshly and fought back, while Ayden just hung his head in dismay and shame. Attacking a king was a death sentence, and only Gabriel's mercy could save either of them now.

Meanwhile, Arthur and Caitlin helped Gabriel and Ashlyn to their feet. With his best friends' aid, Gabriel and his queen-to-be followed Sir Kameran and the rest of the entourage back toward the entrance of the cavern, toward the fading light of day. While he had been fighting for his life, Gabriel realized, the day had passed right by them. He smiled and looked to the sky. *Thank you, Whoever was watching over me*, he thought, *for letting me survive just one more day...*

Upon seeing Solstice, Gabriel smiled and patted the stallion's mane. The horse nudged his injured arm and whinnied worriedly. He reassured his steed that the wounds would heal and that he was all right. Then, with much difficulty and some assistance, Gabriel and Ashlyn climbed into Solstice's saddle, and Gabriel lay along the horse's neck. He was growing weak from the blood loss, but before his consciousness faded, he turned toward the setting sun. Hues of orange and gold shimmered over the water and painted the treetops. The warmth of day was slowly dying off into the coolness of night, and Gabriel smiled slightly as he closed his eyes.

"Don't worry, Gabriel," he heard Ashlyn say to him as she grabbed the reins and ushered Solstice forward, "We're going home."

CHAPTER 15

A NEW REIGN AND AGE

"What were you *thinking*, Sire?!?"

Gabriel cringed inwardly as he endured David Whittenburg's shrill scolding. When they had gotten back to the castle, the young king had been rushed to Sir Dr. Hamilton's apartments for immediate care. Hamilton had cleaned and stitched for close to an hour; all the while, Gabriel had remained unconscious, thankfully, as Hamilton muttered, "Yes indeed, King Gabriel the Scarred."

The wounds on his leg and arm would recover fairly quickly, thanks to the cleansing and powerful medicine that the doctor had concocted. But for now, he was listening to his adviser give him the lecture of a lifetime. After another barrage of wrath, he rolled his eyes and looked away as he sat up in bed, his chest bare and his arm wrapped tightly in white bandages.

"You shouldn't have gone by yourself!" Sir Whittenburg continued harshly. "You could have been killed, Your Highness! Have I not stressed enough how important it is to keep a guard with you? How important *you* are to this kingdom?"

"Enough, David!" Gabriel shouted, causing his adviser to close his mouth with an audible *snap*. Sighing, the youth continued, "I know it was stupid, and I understand what I did was wrong. But if I hadn't done something, Ashlyn wouldn't be here right now! I'm here now, and I'm alive and soon will be healed, so there's no point in lecturing me."

The old man simply shook his head, and also sighed. "From now on, you *must* be more careful. Do you want to end up like your brother, Sire?"

"You tread dangerous waters with that statement, Whittenburg."

The voice was a bit startling; Gabriel and Whittenburg turned quickly to see the source. There in the doorway stood a tall, burly man with pitch-black hair under a gleaming golden coronet, matching ebony facial hair, and a purple robe. His piercing brown eyes were looking upon the elderly scholar in a deadly gaze, making Whittenburg shiver slightly. Gabriel stared as well. "King Peter. Uncle."

The man walked into the room fully and nodded to Whittenburg. Then the burly royal turned to his nephew. "It seems you have been in quite the battle, King Gabriel," King Peter said roughly, making Gabriel turn away and look down slightly.

"Yes... Uncle, I'm—"

"Do not apologize, nephew." The statement made Gabriel turn to King Peter, wide-eyed and shocked. His uncle seemed to understand the astonished/puzzled look on his face, for King Peter simply closed his eyes with a small sigh and pulled up a chair beside the teen royal.

"What happened this evening was not your fault," Gabriel's uncle began, peering at the young king with a stern but understanding look. "I know what my son did, and I know it was wrong. Ayden has caused nothing but trouble for you since your brother's passing, and for that I truly apologize."

The young king turned away slightly, but immediately turned back with an unsettling thought in his head. "Where is Ayden now?" he asked.

"In the dungeons, awaiting your punishment," Peter replied sharply, rising to his feet. "You may decide what to do with him as you will, as is your right as king of this realm. I know I have no right to ask it of you, given what he did, but... I beg you to let him live. His death would devastate your aunt." Peter looked away for a long moment, then looked back to meet Gabriel's eyes. "For now, just rest your body and prepare yourself for your coronation in two days' time," he said.

Again, Gabriel peered curiously at his uncle. "Two days? I thought it was tomorrow."

"With the state you are currently in, it will have to wait a bit," Peter responded flatly as he turned to leave. He was about to push the curtain aside and exit, when he suddenly stopped for a moment, then looked at Gabriel over his shoulder. "You have come a long way from the child you were, Gabriel. I look forward to seeing what kind of king you will be." With that said, the bulky man walked through the velvet door hanging and disappeared.

Gabriel turned back to stare at the wall in front of him, lost in thought. Ayden was locked away, his coronation had been postponed, and he was recovering from near-fatal injuries... He wondered what would become of him now. With the confidence of his uncle and his friends, he felt as though nothing could stand in his way, but he also felt as if he hadn't properly earned what he had achieved. With this troubled thought in mind, he yawned slightly and carefully lay himself back on the cot. Then he closed his eyes and fell deeply asleep.

As he passed into slumber, he realized what was going on with his two best friends, and smiled in his sleep.

Two days passed rather quickly, and Gabriel was back on his feet once again, if not entirely well. He had the strength to stand and walk, though, so the court surgeon had given him the all-clear. Lord Whittenburg said nothing more about his excursion into the woods, and Gabriel even got to see Ashlyn before his important day. Luckily, the dagger hadn't done any real damage to her skin, so she was fine physically; but psychologically, she just wasn't the same. She was a nervous wreck, and she nearly jumped out of her skin whenever someone so much as touched her. Gabriel felt badly about what had happened to her, but he hoped that in time, she would recover and be her old self again, though it might take a while.

On the morning of the ceremony, Gabriel lay in bed, the covers pulled far above his head. He was snoozing happily when he heard a knock on his door and groaned, rolling over on his good side to ignore it. However, the knocking came again, and the young king groaned a little louder, now slightly more awake than he had been. When he didn't answer the door, he heard a long low sigh from the other side. "Sire, please wake up," came Whittenburg's voice through the oak. "It is the day of your coronation. You *must* get up."

Hearing the word 'coronation', Gabriel's eyes shot open and he sat right up straight in bed, wincing at the pain in his injured limbs. "What?! Already?" he cried, hearing a small chuckle in return from the other side of the door. Gabriel leaped from the covers and raced to his closet to look for something to wear. Quickly throwing on an outfit, he rushed to the door and threw it open, to find a grinning Whittenburg standing on the other side.

"My goodness, Your Highness, did you forget?" he chortled, making the teen rub his head sheepishly.

"Maybe..." Gabriel responded.

"Well, let us not waste any more time, Sire," said the old scholar as he turned away from the room. "Your coronation will take place after breakfast, and there is still so much for you to do: we have the final fitting of your ceremonial robes, your coronation speech needs to be perfected still, and you have to make sure that the music for the feast and dance afterward is to your liking."

"I know, I know, David," the youngster replied defensively, smiling a little, "So like you said, let's not waste any more time." Sir Whittenburg beamed, and the two descended the tall decorated staircase to the entrance hall, as regally as a wounded man with a badly injured leg could. Whittenburg provided discreet assistance as needed.

The entrance hall to the keep was bustling with excitement, and filled to the brim with people. It made getting to their destination harder than normal, but Gabriel and his adviser were able to push through the throng of guests and make it to the dining hall, which was also elaborately decorated. Streamers hung along the keystones above them, and the table all bore pure, fresh linens and polished silverware. Gabriel admired the hard work of the servants as he walked to the head of the table and sat down. A delicious meal was placed before him; seasoned scrambled eggs, pan-seared bacon and sausage, flapjacks, and a tall glass of freshly squeezed orange juice—a novelty in mountainous Halcyon Ridge, brought in from hundreds of miles away at great expense. Well, sometimes it was good to be the king. His mouth watered as he eyed the food hungrily.

Then Gabriel grabbed the fork and began to devour the meal in front of him. Whittenburg watched him eat as only a hungry teen male can, before he delved into his own food, though not quite as ravenously.

After they had finished their breakfast, Whittenburg and Gabriel left the crowded hall and walked back toward Gabriel's bedchamber—not to be his for much longer, as he would soon be moving to the suite that had once housed his parents, then his brother and predecessor, Reginald. As they passed a stairwell heading downward, Gabriel looked in the direction of the dungeons, contemplating whether or not to pay his cousin a visit. However, he soon let this thought slip his mind, and continued to follow his adviser up the tall staircase. As they climbed, Gabriel looked out through windows and noted the busyness of the castle courtyards and the town square. Hundreds of guests and other important people had gathered to celebrate, bringing gifts or valuables from their homelands to give to the new king. Gabriel also noticed the stable hands working hard, trying to keep the horses calm, while servants showed the guests into the castle and to their rooms.

He wondered where Ashlyn was, and how she was doing. Would this event with Ayden ruin what they had? He felt a pang of despair at the possibility; he really loved her. He decided firmly that he would wait as long as it took for her to recover.

In town, bakers and chefs were busy preparing meals for the hungry people, while vendors worked to close early so they could attend the coronation. Gabriel stopped for a moment to look upon the town below with a sense of awe and admiration, then hurried to follow Whittenburg.

They reached the top of the tower, and Whittenburg led Gabriel to the summit room, where a few pieces of paper lay on the table at his place. He was supposed to memorize his speech before the event, but he knew that he wouldn't be able to focus at all—though he tried, reciting most if not all of it. He stood before Whittenburg, who pretended to be the audience and coached the young king in what to say and how to sound as regal as possible. After what seemed like a very long time, Gabriel began to get frustrated with it, commenting on his inability to remember any of the words. Whittenburg just smiled and ushered him from the room, assuring him that he would know what to say when the time came.

Just then, the two of them heard the fanfare playing from the throne room, and Gabriel knew that it was time for the coronation to begin. Whittenburg looked up frantically and began to rush down the steps, pushing Gabriel in front of him. "Oh my! We're going to be late!" exclaimed the elderly scholar, "Come, come, Sire! We must get you into your robes! There's no time for a final fitting!"

Gabriel just shook his head with a small grin, which faded fast as anxiety began to settle in his stomach. Would he really know what to say? He didn't have time to worry about it for very long, as they hit the bottom step. The once-crowded room was nearly empty as they sped toward the king's entrance to the throne room. Into the dark hallway the two of them plunged, unnoticed by the sizable group of onlookers that waited outside the oaken archway. Before they reached the velvet curtain that led to the throne room, Whittenburg stopped before another doorway that was also covered in a violet velvet hanging. This room Gabriel hadn't ever noticed before, so he peered at it curiously. He turned to give Whittenburg this same look, but the old man simply cracked a grin and nodded to the door, gesturing for him to walk inside. Gabriel turned back to the door and sighed slightly, then pushed the curtain aside and walked in.

The room was a lot smaller than he had originally thought. Inside, there was a full-length mirror that stood against the left wall, as well as a clothing rack that held nothing except one long, bright red robe, embellished with gold and silver, as well as emeralds and sapphires. It was a robe fit for a king, and as he stood admiring it, Gabriel realized that he was not the only one in the room. He looked up and noticed two ladies who were smiling to him kindly. One was a maid, the very same who had given him water during his fourth trial; the other was Madam Winter. The red-haired seamstress walked up to him with a giant grin and took him by the shoulders.

"Glad to see you made it, Sire," she said as she walked with him to the clothing rack. She then pulled the regal robe from its holder. Gabriel returned her smile.

"I'm happy to be here, Madam Winter," he said.

She grinned broadly and held the regal robe at arm's length. "I am honored to have made this robe for you, Your Highness," she replied gracefully, to which the young man nodded in return.

Gabriel closed his eyes softly as she set the regal cloth gently on his shoulders and fastened it in front. The robe was a bit big for him, but as he opened his eyes again and took a good long look in the mirror at himself, his eyes widened with admiration and awe. He looked stunning; Madam Winter's handiwork was astonishingly elegant and precise. She then circled him once and looked him over, peering at every detail to make sure it was perfect. Satisfied with her work, she beamed and nodded, then sent the teen on his way. Once outside the room, Gabriel could hear the crowd in the throne room chattering loudly, the sound carrying through the hall. He looked toward the king's entrance, only to see his adviser standing there waiting for him with a pile of papers in his hands, as per usual. Gabriel shook his mahogany head and walked up to him. Upon seeing the king, Sir Whittenburg bowed his head respectfully and smiled.

"You look just like your brother, Sire," he said, which made Gabriel's heart both sink and skip a beat slightly. His heart raced again as he heard a fanfare of trumpets being played to silence the growing audience. Whittenburg peeked through the curtain, then he turned back to Gabriel. "Are you ready, Your Majesty?"

"As ready as I'll ever be," replied Gabriel. "I'm not the only one who's been waiting for this day to come. Now that it's here, I just want it to be over with."

"I understand, Sire," the scholar responded, giving him a nod of reassurance before stepping forward to disappear through the velvet door-hanging. The knot in Gabriel's stomach continued to grow as he looked down at his feet. Was he truly ready for this? *Oh, snap out of it, man,* he thought to himself, *You've gotten yourself this far with the help of your friends and supporters... Don't chicken out now.* He shook himself out of his funk just in time to hear Lord Whittenburg say his name. Applause erupted loudly from the throng of guests, and Gabriel knew that it was time.

Swallowing the lump in his throat, he pushed the curtain aside and stepped into the throne room. The crowd cheered even more as they saw their new king enter the room, so much so that the small space seemed to be buzzing with sheer energy. It made Gabriel smile. So many townsfolk and guests from other kingdoms had come to share this moment with him, and he would do his best not to disappoint them. He carefully and gracefully walked to the king's throne, where he spied a small white pedestal that housed the king's royal crown and the royal scepter, only used during ceremonies such as this.

As he faced the throne room door, Gabriel could see everyone in the audience clearly. He immediately spotted his uncle seated in the front row, along with his wife, Lyra, Ayden's mother. Her face was pale, her eyes red, as though she had been crying. He could also see Caitlin and Arthur, who were dressed in the silvery armor of the royal guard. Next to them was Sir Kameran, also in full regalia. In the second row behind them, Gabriel could see Ashlyn. Her long, pale hair had been pulled back slightly into a half ponytail, and she smiled broadly as she saw her future husband step up to the golden chair. On the other side of the room, also in the very first row, were all the members of the Elder Council—except for one, whose name Gabriel couldn't quite remember. There were others that Gabriel recognized as well, but before he could say anything, a hush fell over the crowd. Gabriel turned to Lord Whittenburg to see his hand raised, silencing the audience.

"Citizens of Halcyon Ridge, and distinguished guests," the ivory-haired scholar began, "it is an honor to have you with us here today, to bear witness to and to celebrate the dawning of a new era, a new reign. We thank you for being here to witness the crowning of Halcyon Ridge's new king, Gabriel Alaric Faircross." Gabriel peered about as the audience clapped softly for a few moments, then were hushed again as Whittenburg continued, "We will begin the coronation with the royal ceremonial prayer." Gabriel watched as Lord Alphonse, eldest member of the Elder Council, rose from his seat with a religious text in his hand, and walked up the stage steps until he was in front of the king. Then, the old man opened the dusty old book and turned to a bookmarked page about halfway through.

"Spirit Above," the Elder began shakily, "We pray to thee in this time of glory and joy, to watch over this young lad, for he has an immense responsibility ahead of him..." The man continued, as Gabriel closed his eyes and listened to him speak. While the Elder droned on, Gabriel thought about his new role, and how his brother had once been here, receiving the same blessing. He wondered what Reginald would say if he could see him now... Then he heard the Elder finish the prayer, and opened his eyes. "...And unto him, we pray thee, O Spirit Above, will grant thy blessing and graciousness, for many years to come." The Elder bowed respectfully, and Gabriel nodded in return.

The crowd remained silent as Alphonse walked to the pedestal beside the throne and took up the gleaming crown and scepter. As he slowly stepped in front of Gabriel, the young monarch stared at the golden items, a sense of pride welling up in his chest. Lord Alphonse handed the scepter to him with a small smile. Gabriel took it and grasped it firmly in his left hand, a look of determination in his eyes. Then, the Elder backed away slightly and raised his own left hand.

"Gabriel Alaric Faircross, called the Merciful and the Just based on recent actions," he addressed the young man, "Do you swear to uphold the laws of the realm, and rule this kingdom justly and fairly?"

Gabriel nodded. "I do so swear."

"And do you promise to remain faithful to our country, should it ever be threatened in any way, and to stand with the people in their time of need?"

"I do so promise."

"Then..." A smile crossed the Elder's lips as he raised the crown and steadied it above Gabriel's head, then gently set it upon him. Taking another step back, he knelt on one knee and bowed his head. "...It is with great pleasure that we of the Elder Council of Halcyon Ridge now proclaim you as 24th King of the Realm." Alphonse rose, smiling broadly, and walked back to his seat. He was replaced with David Whittenburg, who beamed proudly and raised a hand into the air, shouting, "Without further ado, ladies and gentlemen, I present to you the Honorable King Gabriel the First!"

"Hail! Hail King Gabriel! Long live the king!" shouted the guests in the traditional response, cheering and clapping for their new ruler. Gabriel's face remained stoic, but inside, his heart leaped and his spirit danced. They were cheering for him; he was now the king! He wished that he could jump for joy, but he remained standing where he was, tall and proud, for all the world to see. He saw Caitlin and Arthur below him, clapping their hardest, as well as King Peter and his wife, with smiles upon their faces; how hard that must have been for Queen Lyra, though she was his mother's sister. He also saw Ashlyn, clapping as hard as she could as tears of joy rose to her emerald eyes.

Gabriel cracked a small smile as he looked them over, his heart filling with love as he looked into Ashlyn's emerald eyes.

Just then, however, there was a loud bang, and the clapping and cheers cut off as everyone stopped immediately and turned toward the sound. The wooden doors to the throne room had been opened and shut, though not quietly. Everyone could now see a lone hooded figure there, dressed in a stained traveler's cloak and faded brown boots. His hands looked worn and rough, and his gait suggested that he was injured; and the throne room was deathly quiet as the man approached the throne. Gabriel's eyes narrowed as he tried to figure out who this person was, though he had a feeling that he was about to find out...

CHAPTER 16

A TALE TO BE TOLD

No one said a word. Not one sound was made as the dark, hooded figure walked the path between the benches toward the throne, toward Gabriel, who peered at him curiously. As he got closer, Gabriel could see the scruffiness of a short, light brown mustache and beard upon the man's chiseled face, though his eyes were hidden under the hood. A sense of familiarity tugged at Gabriel's mind. However, what was more puzzling was the small smile curling across the shadowy individual's lips. He came to a stop a few feet away from the new king. Gabriel could feel a cold sweat run down his spine, but he looked at the man firmly and spoke with as much authority as he could muster: "Who are you? And why have you disrupted this ceremony?" he demanded, his voice booming through the room.

The man didn't seem at all fazed by the king's statement; he simply chuckled a bit. The sound made Gabriel's stomach do flip-flops, and his eyes widened in confusion. *What's going on? What is this feeling?* he wondered.

Then the man dropped to one knee and began to speak. "My apologies, Your Highness," he said respectfully. "I didn't mean to disrupt your coronation. I fear I arrived a bit late." Hushed murmurs filled the air, and even Gabriel held back a gasp. That voice... It was so familiar. Even

Whittenburg stared in astonishment at the newcomer, awaiting his next words. The hooded figure stood once more and put a pale hand to the edge of the hood. It was then that Gabriel spied a golden ring upon the man's ring finger. On it was a familiar insignia; and as he saw it, the teen king swallowed hard.

"No way..." he muttered as he stared wide-eyed at the figure.

The cloak's hood fell behind the mysterious man, and as he looked around the room, all the guests and townsfolk gasped loudly, all of them staring in skeptical bewilderment. Even Lord Whittenburg murmured in disbelief, dropping the parchments in his hand and eying the man in shock. Gabriel said nothing, for he was too busy trying to hold back a flood of tears as the man who stood before him opened his glittering sea-blue eyes and chuckled again, making Gabriel's heart lurch in two different directions.

"I'm sorry for disrupting your celebration, but I had to see my little brother's coronation for myself," Good King Reginald said lightheartedly. "My word, look at how much you've grown!"

Gabriel was rooted to the spot, completely speechless and unable to comprehend what had just occurred. His brother was alive? But how? He had died in battle, or so they had thought, but there the previous monarch stood, alive and well, as if nothing had happened. A mixture of emotions bombarded Gabriel's head, and he did all he could to try and hold himself together. Seeing this look on Gabriel's face, Reginald held his scruffy arms open for his brother. Gabriel took a few steps forward, thinking to himself, *Is this real...? Is it really him...?* Then, the young man broke into a full-force sprint toward his older brother, completely forgetting for a few moments that he was a king. Reginald embraced his younger sibling tightly, allowing the adolescent monarch to sob hard into his dirty clothing. Gabriel cried like no seventeen-year-old boy should have cried, but the overwhelming feelings were too much for him to handle on his own.

"Reggie..." Gabriel uttered through his sobbing. Reginald just held him closer.

"I've missed you, Gabe," the former king responded. Just then,

Whittenburg snapped out of his dumbfounded stupor and walked up to the two of them.

"S-Sire... Your Majesty..." he stuttered, "How is this possible? You were dead! We all assumed—"

"But I wasn't dead, David," Reginald stopped him, pulling the young king away from him for a moment so that he could explain. "It's true the soldiers couldn't find me on the battlefield. It was because I had been captured by the enemy. They also assumed much, thinking that by taking the enemy's king hostage, they would be victorious." Gabriel wiped his eyes as best as he could, then looked up to listen to his brother's tale.

"But then... If you were captured, how did you escape?" the young teen asked.

"I didn't escape," was Reginald's answer. "The Marquis and I had a very long, serious discussion about the possible dangers and outcomes that this war would have, and the conditions of my release. For a while it seemed like he wasn't going to cooperate with me. I was able to finally convince him that in order for the both of us to profit, we needed to work together. So we were able to solve our differences and settled the dispute. He then sent me on my way back to Halcyon Ridge to regain the throne before someone else did—namely the Elder Council." Reginald glanced over at the elders seated in the front row, who had all turned away in utter shame and disappointment; then the former king turned back to Gabriel and Sir Whittenburg.

"When I arrived, however, I could see that preparations already were being made for crowning a new king. I had hoped that they had chosen you, Gabriel, as my successor. I decided to disguise myself as a traveling peddler, so that I could get more information without revealing that I had survived. Sure enough, the townsfolk and people of this kingdom didn't disappoint me, and told me that you were in training to be king." Whispers moved about the crowd of guests as they listened to Reginald's tale. "I returned to the Marquis and told him what had happened, and he seemed a little concerned, as though the deal we had made would turn sour. He then offered me a high position in his own realm, but naturally

I turned him down."

At this point Gabriel gave Reginald a puzzled look and folded his arms over his chest. "But... Why?" he asked.

Reginald looked down at his brother and smiled fondly, placing a hand on his regal shoulder. "Why didn't I take the position?" the former ruler asked. "Because I know where I belong. I knew that you were going to need help, but I didn't want the Elder Council to know that I was alive. If they did, they would have had me reinstated, and all the hard work that you had put into becoming the man you are today would have been for nothing, now wouldn't it?"

As Gabriel looked upon his brother, a mixture of emotions tightened in his chest, and he lowered his head slightly. "So, you had us all believing that you were dead, just so that you wouldn't ruin my chance of becoming king?" he asked tentatively, a slight annoyance in his voice.

Reginald heard this and nodded firmly. "That's correct, Gabriel," he stated.

Although Gabriel knew he should be mad at his brother for pretending to be dead just for his sake, he couldn't bring himself to do it. He was too overwhelmed with this news that he couldn't be mad. Instead, he simply shook his head and clasped his brother's hand in both of his. "You really are something else, you know, Reggie," the current monarch sighed, making the former monarch laugh and smile.

"Ah-hem..." came Sir Whittenburg's voice beside them, making the brothers turn to him as he beamed from ear to ear, "I am pleased to see you alive and well, Your Majesty, but we are in the middle of a coronation..." Reginald's eyes widened in realization and he nodded slightly, turning to Gabriel and bowing respectfully.

"Right, forgive me, I am interrupting your ceremony," he replied, smiling and walking to the front row of seats, where King Peter and his wife made room for him to sit down. They looked just as shocked as everyone else.

"Now then, on with the ceremony," Sir Whittenburg continued, as he and Gabriel returned to the stage. Gabriel stood before the throne once again. It was at this moment he noticed that the scepter on the pedestal had been replaced with a blade, with a golden sheath encrusted with beautiful jewels. It was the ceremonial knighting sword, and he knew exactly who it was for. Smiling, he turned to the audience, as Whittenburg spoke once more, "Caitlin Whitetail and Arthur Darvoux, would you please step forward?"

Gabriel saw his friends rise from the stands, their armor clattering noisily and their faces serious. He watched as they walked up to the stage and stood before him, then knelt on one knee and lowered their heads. Then, Sir Whittenburg took the sword from the pedestal beside the throne and handed it to Gabriel, who took it in his left hand gently. Holding the massive, elegant blade made him feel important. His first act as king would be to knight his friends, and he couldn't be more proud of himself and of them. Smiling, he stepped up to Caitlin and unsheathed the sword, holding it in front of him and closing his eyes.

"Caitlin Whitetail," he began, "For displaying a tremendous act of bravery, I award you with the honor of knighthood." The teen king then lowered the tip of the blade to Caitlin's armored shoulder and tapped it lightly, then he did the same to the other shoulder. Gabriel returned the weapon to its scabbard and walked to Arthur, repeating the process once more. Once the two had been knighted, Gabriel's comrades rose to their feet, and then stood at attention and saluted him. Gabriel smiled and nodded, and the two new knights walked to either side of Gabriel's throne to await further instructions.

Once there, Arthur said nervously, "Um, King Gabriel, is it legal for knights to marry?"

Gabriel lifted an eyebrow. "Of course, Sir Arthur, you know that it is. Dame Caitlin's father is Sir Kameran," he replied.

Sounding exasperated, Caitlin said, "He means is it legal for knights to marry *each other*, Your Highness."

Gabriel blinked. "Well, it's never happened before that I know of," he said slowly. "I mean, there are no female knights—"

"*Ahem,*" Caitlin said loudly, as Arthur reached out to take her hand.

"—until now," Gabriel finished weakly. Then he was struck by an epiphany, like a thunderbolt from the blue. "Oh! Well, that explains a lot! All those times…" he trailed off as his two newest knights of the realm blushed furiously. "Oooooooohhhh. Well, perhaps a double wedding is in order."

Still filled with amazement, Gabriel handed the sword to a servant and returned to his seat.

The room remained silent for a few more moments as everyone peered at the three of them with intense stares, making Gabriel feel a little uneasy for a few moments. Then, the crowd suddenly erupted in a sea of cheers. Their jubilant faces lit up the room, and made the atmosphere more pleasant and joyous. Gabriel grinned slightly at his people, his subjects, those loyal to him by choice, because of his kindness and good judgment. He felt as though his heart would burst from the pride and joy he felt at that moment. Soon, the audience was quieted, and Gabriel knew what would come next; the speech he had prepared before coming to the coronation.

However, just as he was about to say something, his mind went blank, and he forgot his speech in an instant. The young king knew that everyone was waiting to hear him speak, but he didn't have the words to say. He looked to Sir Whittenburg, who was only urging him to go on, but nothing came to mind. Sighing slightly to himself, he puffed out his chest a little and decided to make something up on the fly.

"Thank you all for being here today, honored guests and faithful subjects alike," he began. "I'd like to take this opportunity to appreciate this new role that I have been given. It's a big responsibility, and I wouldn't have made it this far without my support system, both in my friends and family, and in you, the people of this kingdom." The crowd was ablaze with hushed murmurs and whispers yet again, but he continued, "Those who do not live in this kingdom might assume that the only sort of order we have would be relayed through the king himself. Yes, the monarch plays a big part in what goes on here, doing things like making sure there are no food shortages and deciding whether to go to war with another country... But that's not all there is to it. A functional kingdom relies on all the people within it, and those willing to cooperate with the hierarchy, to make the country a better place to live in. Like my brother before me, I plan on ruling this kingdom justly and fairly, with an iron fist when it comes to crime, while lending an ear to those who need it. However, I cannot do it alone. With your support and your help, we can make this kingdom a better place to live, a place where people will see that, should they decide to go to war with us, that they cannot defeat us simply by cutting off the head of the serpent. What happened with Good King Reginald, my esteemed brother, proved that. I vow to do my best and to work together with like-minded people, and perhaps one day, we will see a world that follows suit."

As he finished, yet another roar of excitement arose from the audience. Some of the guests even rose from their seats, clapping and cheering loudly, one of these people being Madam Winter. Gabriel just looked upon the people of his kingdom with a gentle smile. He knew that he was popular with his subjects, and he trusted them.

Just then, Whittenburg stepped forward and made an announcement. "Ladies and gentlemen, there will be an elegant ball this evening in honor of His Highness King Gabriel. We hope to see you there!" Another sea of applause resounded through the room. Soon the excitement died down, and one by one the guests began to file out of the chamber, chattering like songbirds about the events that had unfolded. As soon as the room was seemingly empty, Gabriel sighed heavily and fell to his seat, the gleaming golden crown atop his head sliding over his eyes a little. He had just gotten comfortable when he heard his friends face him. He lifted the crown back into position and looked at them fondly.

"Well, we did it, guys..." he said softly.

His best friends, holding hands again, just smiled. "See? We told you that you could do it, Gabe," Caitlin said cheerfully.

Arthur looked at her rather sternly and shushed her. "Oi, we are to address him as *Your Highness* now, Dame Caitlin," he teased slightly, although his playful grin belied his words. Gabriel couldn't help himself and laughed. Just then, the sound of clanking metal boots echoed about the empty throne room. The King looked up just in time to see Sir Kameran hurrying in.

"Sire! Sire!" cried the panting knight as he halted before the new king, leaning on his knees. Caitlin seemed surprised to see her father, as did everyone else, but Gabriel simply rose from the throne once more and gave him a hard glance.

"What is it, Sir Kameran? You look as though you've seen a ghost."

"Well, with His Majesty's unexpected return, it certainly does feel that way, Sire," the knight captain replied with a bit of humor, but then his expression turned serious, "But that is not why I have come. I regret to inform you that your cousin, Prince Ayden, and his attendant Isabelle have escaped."

Gabriel's eyes widened with worry. "Escaped? How?" he demanded harshly. The other three in the room looked just as shocked.

Sir Kameran only shrugged, but his eyes showed his regret. "I don't really know, Sire," he replied sadly, "But we have determined that the lock to their cell was tampered with."

The thought of his devious cousin on the loose made the young king fall back into his seat, a look of frustration upon his face. *What if he comes for me?* Gabriel thought to himself, *He'll try to take the throne by assassinating me...* Just then he felt a soft, paper-weathered hand come down on his shoulder. As he looked up, he saw Sir Whittenburg there, smiling at him fondly.

"Fear not, Sire, for Ayden can do nothing to you when you have your new guards by your side," he said calmly, gesturing to Caitlin and Arthur. The young monarch looked at the two, who nodded in confidence to him, their hands firmly grasping the hilts of their swords. Then, Gabriel sighed slightly and smiled, a sense of relief washing over him.

"Thank you, all of you. I don't know what I would do without you."

CHAPTER 17

GABRIEL'S RESOLVE

Later that night, it seemed nearly everyone in town gathered in the grand ballroom. The tall ceiling and brightly lit walls were elaborately decorated with banners and tapestries, hanging lights and streamers, making the room seem as if it were glowing. The dance floor had been freshly polished, and long wooden tables of desserts, refreshments, and dinners had been placed against the farthest wall. The folks of the square and royal guests alike were chatting amongst themselves, awaiting the arrival of the new king. Reginald was dressed in his kingly attire, though he didn't have a crown to wear. He stood next to the empty chair that was raised onto a stage near the band—the place where Gabriel would sit once he arrived. Sir Kameran was also dressed nicely, in a kilted suit, but his trusty silver sword wasn't far away, should something untoward occur.

All this Gabriel could see as he peered into the ballroom from outside the door. His expression was one of anxiety, and he pulled himself back to fix the golden crown atop his head. The fringes of his shoulder pads tickled his nose slightly, and the dark blue military-style uniform he had been asked to wear was just a little too small in some places; he'd grown a bit since the original fitting. *What an uncomfortable getup,* he thought, *but if this is what it takes to please my public, then I guess I have no choice.* Sighing to himself softly, he slowly stepped in front of the door, only to be met by the loyal Lord Whittenburg, who had changed from his normal blue starry attire into a long orange robe. His hat was gone as well, revealing places where the long pearly locks were starting to disappear from his head. He smiled upon seeing Gabriel, and bowed deeply.

"Ah, there you are, Your Highness," he said with a grin. "Your subjects await."

With a nod and a quiet "Thank you," the young king entered the room. The warm atmosphere made him smile, as did seeing the townspeople dancing and having a good time. As soon as they noticed him, everyone in the room began to cheer and clap for their king; as they music trailed off, they parted to one side, leaving a small path leading to the raised throne, and Gabriel walked toward it, nodding to those who praised him along the way. He recognized many of those in the crowd; one was Madam Winter, who was wearing a brand-new dress that she had made specifically for the coronation ball. Two others were Caitlin and Arthur, who waved to him as he passed. Arthur wore a rust-colored suit complete with medium length coat-tails, while Caitlin wore a navy-blue gown that reached the floor. Her brilliant blonde hair had been tied up in a tight ponytail, fastened with a small bow. Gabriel smiled as he saw them, and their linked hands, then continued on his way. Once he had reached the raised stage, he looked to Reginald, who just smiled and nodded to him respectfully. Then, the new monarch of Halcyon Ridge turned to face his people. Whittenburg appeared by his side. "Announcing his Royal Highness, King Gabriel Faircross the First, Monarch of Halcyon Ridge," he stated, his voice booming through the room. Once again, the room was ablaze with excitement.

Not long after, the room had settled down a bit, and the guests were chattering with each other once again. Caitlin and Arthur mingled with the townsfolk, who congratulated them on their success. Sir Kameran kept a keen eye on everyone, making sure nothing went wrong, while Whittenburg spoke with a few of the aristocrats who had come. They looked like they were speaking about something important. Reginald stood beside Gabriel the entire time, looking at his brother in fondness and pride.

As Gabriel settled in his chair, a servant brought him food and refreshments. He then scanned the crowd once again; there was one person he'd been looking forward to seeing, but she wasn't there yet. It was then that Gabriel looked up at his elder sibling. "Reggie, where's Ashlyn?" he asked curiously.

Reginald smiled, patting his younger brother's back gently. "Your young lady is still getting ready," he replied, turning toward the door. "She'll be here shortly."

No sooner had he said it than a hush fell across the room. Standing in the doorway to the ballroom was a stunningly beautiful young woman; Gabriel's eyes widened and his jaw dropped as he stared at her in awe. She was dressed in a pale pink satin ball gown, with puffed out shoulders and lace fringe along the hem. Rosy red bows held her straw-colored hair in a tight bun atop her head, and she was crowned by an elegant silvery tiara encrusted with diamonds and sapphires; it had been Gabriel's mother's, and he recognized it at once. Her shy smile and bright green eyes lit up the room, and her high-heeled shoes echoed as she strode in gracefully, her hands folded neatly in front of her.

The more he gazed upon her, the more Gabriel smiled and told himself that he had made the right choice. She was astonishing, gorgeous beyond compare, as well as extremely brave, intelligent, and just... wondrous.

The crowd parted once again to allow Ashlyn to make her way to the king. Murmurs of wonder and admiration reverberated across the room, as the people commented on their future queen's marvelous beauty. As she reached the stage where Gabriel sat, she smiled fondly to him and unfolded her hands, curtsying to him daintily. Gabriel himself beamed brightly and rose from his seat, walking to her. It was then that Ashlyn looked about the room, noticing the stares she was receiving, and a hint of pink blush crawled across her nose. "Oh my..." she muttered in embarrassment, "I-I didn't mean to cause a scene..."

Gabriel only took her hands in his own, making her twirl back to face him. "Let them stare," he said softly, "because they've never seen anything like you in their lives." She blushed profusely, making him smile. "Ash, you look amazing tonight."

The timid grin returned and Ashlyn giggled a little, turning away from him slightly. Just then, the band began to play a slow melody, perfect for a couple's dance. As if in silent communication, everyone cleared a spot for the two of them in the middle of the floor, which Gabriel took full advantage of. He let go of her hands and stepped back, bowing to her and holding out his hand. "May I have this dance, my lady?"

Ashlyn giggled once again. "Why yes, Your Majesty," she replied with another curtsy. "I would be honored."

Ashlyn grasped Gabriel's outstretched hand, and then the king led his future queen to the center of the cherry-wood floor and pulled her in close. His right hand held her left, and his left hand rested gently upon her hip, while she placed her right hand on his tasseled shoulder. The music drifted through the grand hall, and with a small nod, Gabriel led them in a waltz. Round and round the two twirled and danced, swaying to the beat and gliding effortlessly across the dance floor. They pranced by many an aristocrat, who shot glances of awe and admiration at the two. Seeing them stare, Ashlyn blushed even more and her timid smile faded a little; Gabriel rested his forehead on hers gently and beamed fondly. Following his lead, Ashlyn smiled back and seemed to forget about the gawking crowd. Not once did the two make a mistake, and time seemed to slip away as they glided across the room, making the men grin and the women sigh happily.

Then, all too soon, the music came to a gentle stop, and soft clapping echoed about for the two teens. They smiled at each other once again, bowing to each other courteously. Then, the two returned to the raised stage where Reginald still stood, and everyone else crowded the center of the room once more. As Gabriel returned to his seat, Ashlyn smiled and laughed softly.

"You are very skillful as a dancer, Sire," came his adviser's voice from his left.

Gabriel turned to him and chuckled a little. "Hey, I can be nimble and graceful when I want to be, David," he teased. Ashlyn blushed again and grinned widely.

It was then that the knight captain and his two new knights walked up, bowing to their king. "You two were so elegant out there!" Caitlin complimented, making even Gabriel blush a little.

"Hah, thanks."

"So, Gabe... Um... I mean, Sire..." Arthur corrected himself quickly as he received a piercing glance from Whittenburg, "When are you going to tell everyone?"

Whittenburg, Sir Kameran, and Reginald looked at the four teens in confusion. "What does he mean?" Sir Kameran asked, but Reginald only grinned and chuckled.

"I think I know," he said with a wry smile as he turned to his younger brother. "It's about your future queen, right?" Gabriel gave his sibling an astonished look. However, as he turned back to the others, Arthur nodded. Caitlin just beamed happily, while Ashlyn turned red-faced.

"Yes," Gabriel responded as he faced his adviser and the middle-aged knight. "As you could probably tell, I have chosen my queen. I chose Ashlyn. She has already agreed to marry me."

Gabriel was expecting the two of them to give him looks of shock or confusion. However, instead, the two of them simply beamed and laughed happily, giving each other small understanding nods before turning back to the king. "Well, we had an idea she was who you would choose," Sir Kameran told him.

"She seems to have wholeheartedly captured your heart, Sire," Lord Whittenburg agreed.

Gabriel blushed slightly and smiled, looking at his friends and biggest supporters. "Thank you. Truly, I don't know what I would have done if it weren't for you..."

"Aw, come on, Your Highness," Caitlin retorted cheerfully, "You did most of this on your own."

"Yeah, we just made you see that you can believe in yourself," Arthur agreed with a nod.

"You merely had to find your own courage and strengths for yourself, Sire," Whittenburg chimed in.

"Your friends and followers believed in you the whole time, Gabriel," his brother said gently. "The question now is, do you believe in yourself as much as they do?"

Gabriel turned away from them all for a moment to think. His brother did bring up a good point... But he already knew the answer, and turned back to Reginald with a determined nod. "I know I do," he responded. His elder sibling returned his nod and grinned. Then, Gabriel turned to them all once more and started chatting with his friends. Their words were kind and playful. Gabriel was happy to be able to marry the girl he loved; he was surrounded by people who loved him as well, and for that, he was truly grateful.

From that moment on, Gabriel ruled the kingdom as he saw fit. He was kind yet stern, just and fair, yet understanding and generous. He proved to be an excellent king indeed. He still had a lot to learn, and much to gain from his experiences, but he had his supporters, his friends, his fiancée, and his only living family once more. He was more than confident that he could handle anything that life could throw at him. His wedding was postponed due to his lessons, as well as the normal royal duties as king, but Gabriel was determined to marry Ashlyn. Reginald was not reinstated, at his own insistence, but instead was given a place on the Elder Council. The gathering of elderly men and women still didn't seem thrilled about his unexpected return, but they welcomed him nonetheless.

One morning, about a month after his coronation, Gabriel sat in the throne room, listening to issues that the townspeople had brought to his attention. Caitlin and Arthur stood beside his chair, guarding him, brand new silver swords hanging at their hips. As the last group of people exited through the tall oaken archway, Gabriel sighed and leaned back in his seat. It had been a long day already, and he was looking forward to some lunch. Caitlin and Arthur stepped in front of him and smiled.

"Looks like we're finished," Arthur said happily.

"How about we go get some food?"

"Sounds great," the king replied, and stood up to leave. Just then, however, the sound of footsteps echoed in the hall, and the three turned to see who had come.

"Excuse me, Your Highness," the man who entered said with a smile. He wore a white robe with gold and red embroidery at the seams. "May I have a word with the King? Alone?" After his two guards and he exchanged a glance, Gabriel shrugged and sent them on their way with a smile.

"We'll be right outside, Sire. Please call if you need us," Caitlin told him, and then the two of them exited through the velvet curtain behind the thrones, leaving the two men alone.

Gabriel turned to his elder sibling and walked down the steps of the stage toward him. It had only been a month, but to him it still didn't seem possible that Reginald was alive. Seven years had passed as the war dragged on; Gabriel had been depressed and lonesome for a long time, but seeing the previous ruler here and now made him feel much better, and a lot more confident than he ever had been. As he reached the bottom step, he walked up to Reginald and embraced him tightly.

Reginald just smiled and returned the gesture. "Hello, brother," the former king sighed fondly, and released Gabriel gently.

"Hello, Reggie. It's so good to have you back. I'm still amazed you were alive all that time."

"It's good to be back," Reginald replied happily. He looked past Gabriel toward the stage where the thrones sat, and smiled fondly, "To think, it was seven years ago that I stood here and told you that you would be king one day. And here you are, making my statement a reality."

"Yeah, it wasn't easy, but I suppose I proved myself worthy in the end."

"Indeed you did," Reginald replied.

"So, what brings you down here? How are things going with the Elder Council?" Gabriel asked.

Reginald shrugged. "Could be better. Believe it or not, there was a lot of corruption and coercion going on without either of us knowing."

"What do you mean?" Gabriel asked, peering at his brother in puzzlement.

"The Elder Council was afraid of one man and his influence, and therefore they did as that person wanted," Reginald stated, crossing his ivory-clothed arms in front of his chest. "William Reidfield. Does the name ring a bell?"

Gabriel rubbed his chin in thought for a moment, trying to think of where he had heard the name before. Suddenly, it clicked. "Isabelle, Ayden's attendant!" he exclaimed, "Is he related to her somehow?"

"He's her father," Reginald replied with a nod.

"Oh..."

"His influence made him seem like a powerful man, but he isn't really," Gabriel's older brother continued. "He was the reason Ayden was able to get into all of your tournaments and try to best you. He used the fear that he had instilled in the others to get his way. He would have given the throne to Ayden if the others hadn't stopped him."

"How did you find this all out?" Gabriel asked.

Reginald smirked. "The knight captain's daughter has her ways..."

"Like father, like daughter, I suppose," Gabriel teased. The two of them laughed.

Then Reginald continued, "Ah, but I am keeping you from your duties... and your lunch."

"It's all right. I always have time for family."

"You know, Gabriel," Reginald began, as they strode toward the throne. They stopped to regard the large portrait on the wall behind the dais, which still displayed the image of their parents and their younger selves. "I can say with certainty that Mom and Dad would have been very proud of you. I am too. I'm proud of the man that you've become, and I'm honored to have you as family—and as my king."

The young monarch felt his chest becoming tight. Hearing those words from his brother made his sense of pride swell even more than it had, and the teenager smiled broadly. "Thanks, brother... It means a lot to me to hear you say that."

"Of course. That's what family is for, you know."

"I do know."

The two of them exchanged one more glance, then they both left through the king's entrance. Their future looked bright at last. Gabriel knew that it was only just the beginning of his reign, but he knew also that it was the start of something more: a revolutionary period that would change their kingdom forever. He would rule the lands with total inflexibility when it came to crime, but otherwise he would be kind and generous, like his brother and parents before him. On top of that, he would have the woman he loved ruling by his side, his best friends protecting him always, and the strength of his subjects and supporters from other realms. All these things made him feel empowered to do what was right. Gabriel knew he would have a lot more challenges to face later, but he would face them head on, no matter what came. He had finally stepped out of his brother's shadow, and was now living his life on his own—as the king he had always been destined to become.

ABOUT THE AUTHOR

Lacey Marie Leach was born and raised in rural Maine and currently lives in Blue Hill, Maine, working as a baker.

Leach has been writing since the young age of thirteen, and as she grew older, she dreamt of publishing a novel. While she has many unfinished works, *In My Brother's Shadow* is her first published novel. The inspiration behind the book were her two young children, Gabriel and Kahlan, as well as Disney's *Frozen* and *Robin Hood*.

www.ingramcontent.com/pod-product-compliance
Lightning Source LLC
Chambersburg PA
CBHW020959180626
46814CB00003B/1162